Pond Puckster

Pond Puckster

Mark Fidler

BLR Books
Belmont, Massachusetts

Pond Puckster

BLR Books
163
464 Common Street
Belmont, MA 02478

ISBN: 0-9721839-0-6

Thanks to my wife Tobey and my friend Rob
for their editorial assistance

For Leland

Prologue

Number 5 accelerated at the red line, one teammate to his right, one man to beat. The deafening roar of the crowd almost drowned out the words of the excited announcer.

"It's Quinn with the puck, 2-on-1! The master of the play!"

Quinn, Number 5 for the Black Bears, shoveled a crisp pass to his wing. The wing instantly yanked back his stick and leaned his whole body into the puck, firing a slap shot past the defenseman and at the goal. Fifteen thousand fans screamed.

With lightening-like reflexes, the goalie shot out his right pad and kicked out the puck. "Save!" screamed the announcer.

In a fraction of a second, Number 5 was on the loose puck and without a moment's hesitation he flicked the puck over the goalie's leg pad and the red light flashed on.

"Score! Jason Quinn!"

The crowd erupted. The entire Black Bear team spilled out onto the ice and smothered their captain and star. It was minutes before the words of the announcer could be heard.

"Jason Quinn with an upper corner goal on the rebound! What a way for the six foot two senior to end an amazing four year career for the University of Maine! All they have to do now is hold on for the next eighteen seconds and the Black Bears from Maine will be the new national college champions. Ladies and gentleman, this is the most exciting moment in hockey that I've ever seen."

I squirmed as the image on the large screen disappeared and the lights went on in the cavernous auditorium. I always felt a little uncomfortable whenever I looked at a film of myself. On the stage and below the screen, a middle aged man in a deep blue suit spoke into a microphone at the podium. It was a man that I knew quite well.

"I don't have to tell you what happened next," the man said to the audience. "Every time I see that tape, I get swept away by the drama. And I've seen it many times. Wow! What a moment! And so it gives me great pleasure to present this year's Distinguished Alumni Athletic Award to Number 5 of that championship squad."

The speaker paused as the crowd cheered.

"Jason Quinn was captain of that great Black Bear team," the well groomed man in the blue suit continued. "In his four years at the University of Maine he became the third leading scorer in the University's history, with 86 goals and a Black Bear record of 139 assists. Impressive statistics. But more than that, Jason Quinn was and is a first class individual. He is a team player all the way. Not only does he have the Black Bear record for assists, but I have never known a player to spend more time helping his teammates with their game. Words of encouragement, friendly, smart advice and even extra sessions with younger players at six o'clock in the morning. I can't say enough about this man. After fifteen years as Athletic Director and numerous others as a coach and player, I can tell you this: they don't come any better than Jason Quinn. Students, alumni and friends of the University, this year's Distinguished Alumni Athletic Award recipient, Jason Anderson Quinn!"

A thousand people rose as one, cheering and whistling and screaming. I was in tears. My legs shook as I walked up to the podium and grasped Athletic Director Miller's right hand. I was overwhelmed with emotion. I turned and faced the cheering audience. There were so many faces I knew, so many people I loved. But it was the others, all those screaming people I didn't recognize, who took my breath away. I was moved that I had touched their lives so deeply.

I didn't have a prepared speech. I'm not very good at reading speeches. I'd much rather speak directly to the people. And so, when they finally quieted down, I spoke to them. I can't remember much of what I said. My Aunt Susan taped it, but every time she wants to show it, I get too embarrassed and insist she do it another time. I'm sure I talked about the great players on that team, and about my phenomenal coach. I expect that I talked about teamwork and goals and hard work. And I know I talked about the fun of playing the game.

Afterwards there was a question and answer session, and a teenage boy asked me what person or experience was the biggest influence in my life as a hockey player. That was a tough one. I thought for a long time, and everyone was still. I remembered so many moments that had helped to make me the player and person I am today. I saw the faces of countless people in that journey. And as my mind fast-forwarded through these memories, I realized that most of them came from one year of my life, one hockey season, one winter. There was too much for me to share right then, but later in the night and all the next day, I thought about that winter. I relived it.

What did have the biggest impact on my life and my hockey career? All I said in answer to the boy's question was, "It was the winter when I was ten years old. It was my winter on Spy Pond in Glenville, Maine."

Chapter 1

"PASS IT!" DARYL screamed from my right.

I glanced up in front of me and saw just one Ranger defenseman. My blue jerseyed opponent was skating backwards, directly between me and the goal. I can do it, I thought. I can beat him. I pivoted hard off my right skate and crossed it over my left, with the puck still on my stick. I moved my legs as fast as I could. It was an incredible feeling, skating this fast and this smoothly over the ice. It almost felt like I had wings. I rounded my opponent and cut back in toward the goal, keeping my eyes glued to the puck as I stick-handled. A second later, I looked up and there was the goalie right in front of me! Without thinking, I fired the puck and heard the smack as it ricocheted off the goalie's stick and into the corner. I had been too close to the goalie when I shot it. I had skated with my head down. It was a mistake and I knew it.

Daryl was in the corner digging for the loose puck. I skated in front of the goal and positioned myself to receive a pass. Daryl fought an opponent and skated out with the puck. He saw me wide open and slid the puck in front of their goalie, right toward my stick. The Ranger goalie dove out of the crease and trapped the puck on the ice with his outstretched catching mitt and the referee blew the whistle. I glanced at the bench and saw my coach signaling a line change. I looked up at the clock. 1:48 remaining in the game. Darn! No way would I get back in.

I skated back to the bench with my head hung low. Coach Tower held the door open as my line of five skaters stepped up off the ice. I took my place on the bench and stared down at the strips of hard, black mat pieced together like a jigsaw puzzle.

Two hands clamped down on my shoulders from behind. "How many times have I said 'pass the puck?' "

I said nothing.

"We're a team, Jason. It doesn't matter who scores the goal. It's how we do that matters."

Sure, I thought. What world is he living in? Most kids care more about goals, assists and ice time. Even the coaches will cut a guy at the end of the season if a better kid comes along.

"Well, Jason?"

"I thought I could beat him, Coach."

"You did beat him, but by the time you were around him, you had no angle. That's why you pass in a two-on-one situation like that."

The coach was probably right, but I knew that I was a better hockey player than Daryl. That's why I hadn't passed it. I was replaying the move in my head, not even watching the game, when Andy, our goaltender, came tumbling over the boards, landing on my lap!

"Quinn, move!" one of the coaches hollered.

I was confused, wondering what our goalie was doing off the ice. Suddenly everyone on the Terrier bench was up and screaming. Shawn Keefe had scored the tying goal! The coach must have pulled the goalie and sent an extra skater on the ice. The other five Terrier skaters were piled on top of Shawn while the crowd and my teammates howled and cheered with joy.

That could be me they're jumping on, I thought angrily. I should be the star of the moment. I should have tried deking the goalie.

Andy shuffled in front of me and stepped out the door, back onto the ice. The score was locked, 3 - 3. I hoped that my coach would put my line back on to try to win it. I still could be the hero. But Shawn's line stayed on the ice while Coach Tower and Coach Mackey continued clapping.

I just stared at the clock as the seconds ticked away, and then the game was over. Both teams skated onto the ice and lined up for the handshake. I barely held out my glove while the Ranger players each tapped it with one of their own, most mumbling, "Good game."

I skated off the ice right behind Daryl.

"You should have passed to me," Daryl snarled as he tromped in his skates over the wet mat to our team room.

I said nothing. I wanted to tell Daryl that I didn't pass because he had a lousy shot, but I didn't say anything. Daryl wasn't very quick on the ice, but he was bigger than me and pretty tough, too. I was a little afraid of him.

"Great game, you guys. Great comeback! Great *team* effort!" Coach Tower said as we entered the team room.

I didn't even look up at my coaches as I walked to my spot on the bench. While other kids were unsnapping their helmets and starting to untie their skates, I sat motionless.

"Nice game, Jason," a familiar voice said to me.

I finally looked up to the smiling face of my mother.

"I was lousy."

"But you guys tied the game. That was so exciting!"

"Yeah, sure Mom."

"What's wrong with you? You were awesome," she said and paused, "even if you should have passed the puck that last shift," she continued in a hushed tone.

"You don't know what you're talking about!" I snapped loudly. The boys and parents near me stopped talking while they awkwardly looked away.

"Enough!" my mother whispered harshly. "Listen, there's something I need to tell you."

"I don't want to hear anything!" I insisted in a loud whisper.

"Listen, Jason, it's important. I wanted to tell you before the game, but I thought it might ruin it for you, so I waited -"

"Mom, I said that I don't want to hear it!" I interrupted, my voice rising again.

"But Jason, I have to tell you -"

"Team!" Coach Tower's voice boomed over the clatter. People quieted down. "I have an important announcement to make. This is Jason's last game with our team. He and his mother are moving to Maine this week. They just found out, and so this is it. We'll certainly miss you, Jason, but there's some lucky team up north who will be getting you, I'm sure."

I was speechless. I looked at my mother in bewilderment. She forced a smile to her face and shrugged her shoulders.

"Mom?" was all I could say.

"I tried to tell you, Jason," she whispered. "I'm sorry. I just found out yesterday. We have to be out of the house by Saturday. I didn't want this to happen, but it did."

No more playing hockey with the Junior Terriers? They were the best select team in the league and one of the best in New England! It was only September, and the season had just begun. It couldn't be! I had been waiting to make this team for two years. As a ten-year-old, this was my last year in the Squirts, and I had finally been selected for the Terriers. And my other team, my town team, had nine guys returning and was supposed to be one of the best in the Greater Boston League. I was counting on playing for two championship teams! This couldn't be true!

I found myself standing with my white high-tops on. I hadn't even noticed that my mother had taken off my skates and put on my sneakers. It didn't matter. Nothing mattered anymore. I barely heard the other guys say good-bye as my mother led me out of the skate room.

Chapter 2

"WHY DO WE HAVE to move?"

"Jason, the traffic's real bad. Let's talk about it when we get home." My mother adjusted the rear view mirror and glanced quickly at it.

"Aren't you going too fast, Mom?" I said in a critical tone of voice.

My mother stared straight through the windshield and said nothing.

"Mom, I said you're driving too fast!" I snapped.

My mother continued to ignore me. How could she make me move away? It wasn't fair. And now she wouldn't even talk to me! This is what she used to be like with Dad, I thought. They'd fight, he'd yell at her, and she would ignore him. I used to mostly side with my mother in those arguments, but now I was so mad at her, I thought that my father had probably been right.

"Slow down!" I commanded. I remembered how much it used to bother my mother when my father criticized her driving.

She squeezed the steering wheel tighter but didn't say a word.

"Mom!"

My mother reached down and clicked on the car radio, jerking the volume up high. A surfing song by the Beach Boys blared from our four car speakers. With the push of a button I opened my window, and I stuck my head out and screamed, "My mom's driving bad and is gonna kill me! Help!"

She jammed on the brakes, causing me to bump my head against the side of the window.

"Jason Anderson Quinn, you shut your mouth this instant or I'll throw you out of the car!" she screamed while turning down the radio. Her shrill voice rang in my ears and stunned me. I said nothing but still glared at her defiantly.

She paused, breathed deeply, and continued in a calmer voice. "I can't do this, Jason. Please don't push me. I don't know what I'll do if you don't stop."

"But why do we have to move?"

"It's your father's fault."

"But Dad's dead!"

We were both speechless. I had said it. Dead. I think that it was the first time I actually spoken the word. I had tried to think of him as just not being around. Before he died, he was usually so busy with work that I hardly ever saw him anyway. I had told myself that things weren't much different now, but they were different and I knew it. At that instant, I wasn't angry with him. I just missed him.

"Why is it Dad's fault?" I asked quietly.

"Before he died, he did a lot of things in his business that might not have been right. They're tying up all our assets while it gets resolved."

"What does that mean?" I asked.

"It means that we don't have any money, and we can't even keep on paying for our house. We have to leave, and the bank is going to sell it. And we might not even get any of the money because your dad may have owed more money than he was telling us. Jason, I don't want to leave any more than you do, but we don't have any choice."

"What about *your* job?"

"*My* job doesn't pay money. It's a volunteer position at the museum."

"You don't make any money at your work? Then why do you do it?"

"Your father made more than enough money. I used to be a nurse's aid, remember? I've told you that I quit when we got married. I couldn't stand working weekends and holidays, and the money was terrible. Then, somehow, I got connected at the museum. I loved getting out and meeting the people and just being around the artwork. But it won't pay the bills now."

"Why can't you get a nurse's job again? Then we could still live here!"

"No one can live in these parts on what I'd make as a nurse's aid. Plus, I'm going to be very busy trying to straighten up your father's affairs. I need someone to help look after you."

"Where are we going to live?"

"We're going to move way up to Glenville in with your Aunt Susan and Uncle John for a while."

"But the Reeses have six kids! There won't be room for us!"

"With six kids, what's one or two more?"

"But I don't like those kids, Mom."

"They're your cousins, Jason."

"I still don't like them."

"You hardly know them. They're doing us a big favor. We can't exactly be choosy."

"Can I play on a hockey team up there?"

"I have no idea. I don't even know if there's a rink up there. And I don't know how expensive it is. We have to find out."

There might not be a hockey team? I felt sick at the thought. There had to be one! Hockey was the only thing that I liked to do. School was boring, I didn't have many friends, and TV and videos got monotonous after a while, too. Hockey was the only thing I loved. And this year I was playing on both my town team plus a select team. I had to play on a team!

"What about my Christmas present?"

"Huh?" my mother asked.

"The Canadian Hockey Tour, with the Northeast Eagles, you know, that All-Star team I made. I can still do that, can't I?"

"I don't know. I don't think so. It's a lot of money. I'm sorry."
Mom looked sadly at me.

"Then I'm not going to ask *you*. I'm going to ask Santa Claus
for that. So you don't have to pay for it," I declared, staring
defiantly at my mother.

Mom raised her eyebrows and gave me a 'come on' look. She
opened her mouth to say something but suddenly looked
unsure, and just said, "Uh, Jason, uh, Santa doesn't always get
everything a kid wants."

"He always has with me. Last year I asked for a week of
skiing at Big Mount resort, and I got it. And that was a pretty
big thing. And the year before I got a brand new computer. I've
always gotten the big thing that I asked for."

"This year might be different."

"How do you know?"

My mother had never told me whether or not Santa was real.
For the past two years, she had acted as if I knew the truth, but
nothing was ever said. It now seemed like a good time to talk to
my mother as if I did believe in him. This present was one that I
wanted more than any other that I had ever asked for. Even
though I was ten years old, I thought that playing the Santa
Claus card might just work.

My mother seemed to struggle to find the right words. Finally
she looked me right in the eye and said quietly, "I just don't
want you to be disappointed, Jason. Can I drive now?"

"Yeah," I mumbled.

Chapter 3

MY EYES DANCED FROM one treasured item to another in my room. My room. This would be the last night that I would ever sleep here. Toys and games were strewn over the floor. Two large cartons in the middle of the room were overflowing with clothes, toys and hockey equipment. One other sat empty.

Why did my mother say that I could only bring three cartons full of things? I didn't remember Aunt Susan's and Uncle John's house being that small. I didn't remember it being big either. I had been only seven when we last visited, and all I really remembered was lots of kids and lots of noise. My mom had said that they were crowded in a tiny house, and that I could only bring these three cartons of stuff with me. At first, I had filled all three cartons with toys and hockey equipment, but my mom said that I had to pick out the clothes I wanted and include them in those cartons. And if I didn't choose enough clothes, then she would throw out toys to make room for what I needed to wear. And so I had dumped everything out of the cartons, picked out my favorite clothes and put them in one carton. They filled the first one. I then threw my hockey bag with all my equipment in a second. If I couldn't decide what to put in the third carton, I could wait until the next morning. My father always used to say that it was important to "sleep on it" before making an important decision.

On the floor in front of my dresser was an automatic nerf-ball blaster. It had been a birthday present, one that I had asked for. It was cool, but without anyone to shoot, it hadn't been as much fun as I had hoped. I didn't have any brothers or sisters, and I hadn't often had any friends come over. But six cousins could make pretty good targets. Maybe I should take it. Or maybe my

Super-Water-Rifle would be better. That was another toy I had never used much. There was that hot afternoon in the summer when I had chased my father around the yard with it and gotten him really good. I had hidden in a tree and waited until my parents stretched out in their yard chairs to read. Then pow! Dad had screamed that his book was ruined, and Mom had just plain screamed. It was great. They had told me to stop, but I didn't. I remembered just squirting and squirting until my father actually began to climb the tree coming up after me! I kept on firing until he was an arms length away, still hollering.

"Give me the gun!" he demanded.

I knew that he was really mad, and so I did finally give him the Super-Water-Rifle. My dad took it, climbed down the tree and stormed into the house with the rifle. I can still see the image of my father flying out the door a few minutes later, hooting like an Apache warrior, and firing the Super-Water-Rifle at me as I was swinging down from the bottom branch of the tree. At first, I had been scared when I saw an angry, mean look in his eyes, but within a minute, my dad was running down the long hill in our yard, firing water at me, and we were both laughing. When the water ran out, Dad even let me fill it up again and chase him around the yard and try to shoot him.

I smiled at that good memory. But I was sad, too. That was the only time I could remember playing with my father like he was a kid. I hardly remembered laughing with him at all. My dad was almost never home. He spent most of his time at work, and traveled a lot on his job. For vacations, my parents usually flew to an island by themselves and left me with whatever nanny I had at the time. They did take me on that ski vacation that I had asked Santa for, but I didn't see them too much that week either. They skied themselves all day and left me with the "Ski Tots" instructors. I loved skiing, so that had been okay, and we did all eat dinner each night at a restaurant, and my parents let me stay up in our hotel room as late as I wanted to watch TV.

Maybe if my father were still alive, he might have done more fun things like squirt gun fights. At that second, I missed him a lot.

I looked to the other side of my room, near my desk. There was a pile of action figures and fighters of every kind. Robots, aliens, soldiers, super-heroes, monsters. They were of all colors, shapes and sizes. When I was younger, they had been my favorite toys. There were some great wars back then. I didn't spend much time with them anymore, but it didn't feel right to leave them all here. The stuff I didn't take would mostly go into storage, my mom had said. Someday I'd get it all back. I wasn't exactly sure what 'storage' was. What if some other kid saw my stuff and just took it? I thought that if I really wanted something, I'd better take it now.

There was a whole shelf of games that I had gotten as gifts but had never played. Some still looked like fun, but a kid can't play them by himself. My parents never had time for games. My father always said that someone had to earn the money to buy that stuff. Once I had said to my father, "Who cares, if you never have time to play them with me." My mother had said that it's a Catch-22, which is an impossible situation where you always lose. Parents who don't work hard have time to play with their kids, but they don't have money to buy fun things to play with. Parents who do spend most of their time working can buy great things but don't have time to enjoy them with their kids.

I wondered what kind of people my uncle and aunt were. Did they have time to play with their kids or the money to buy stuff with? I hoped that they had the money because with all my cousins, who needed parents to play with? That would be the best thing, I thought. Parents to buy good toys and lots of brothers and sisters to play with.

In another corner of the room was a pile of sports equipment, mostly old hockey gear. I wouldn't need that. A lot of it was cheap stuff or didn't fit. Until I was seven, I didn't really know the equipment to buy, and so some of my old stuff was good and some of it was lousy. When I was six, my skates were terrible, and I wasn't able to skate right. My ankles caved in like a saggy tent just standing on the ice. Finally a coach told my parents to get a better pair of skates for me. My parents had already bought the best pair in the store, but the problem was that they had gone to a department store. You don't buy skates in a department store! They thought that thirty bucks was a lot to pay for skates and that they were good ones, because when they were little, you paid about five dollars for a pair. I remembered that day they brought me to Murray's Sporting Goods for my first decent skates. The guy showed them a pair that cost more than one hundred dollars. My mother's eyes almost popped out of her head, but my father just handed over his credit card. Those were size ones and too small now, and they sat on the floor next to the cheap skates. 'Cheap skates.' That was an expression that my father used to use when he talked about a lot of people. Well, the two pairs don't belong in the same pile, I thought, almost sneering at those old, stupid skates.

My first pair of hockey socks was in the heap, too. They were maroon and white but not very white, more like gray, and there were more holes than sock in them. My mother had wanted to throw them out, but I wouldn't let her. If I became a famous hockey player, those things might be in the Hockey Hall of Fame. Or maybe I could sell them for a lot of money. Definitely! I couldn't decide whether I should bring those old leggings with me to my cousins' house. If I left them in storage, maybe someone would steal them. It would be a tough decision. There were also old shoulder pads and shin pads and hockey pants. My first pair of gloves was there too. They were blue and had holes in the palms, but they had been good gloves. At first they had been stiff, and I found it hard to just hold my stick with them on. After a while, though, they became soft and awesome. I hadn't even wanted new ones, but my father had insisted, saying that people would think we were poor if I wore those beat up old things.

Mixed in with my old hockey equipment were all-leather baseball gloves, super light aluminum bats and two pairs of almost new soccer cleats. I wasn't very good at baseball and soccer, and a year ago I had quit playing them completely. Baseball was too slow and boring, and I was afraid to move up to the "kid pitch" league. Billy Mahoney, who was a year older and lived near me, had been beaned by a fastball and had broken his nose. For three weeks he had looked like a monster in school with purple circles around his eyes and his nose bandaged like Freddy Krueger's mask. And soccer had too much running for me. Skating was a lot more fun. No, I wouldn't bother bringing any old baseball or soccer things.

Right next to the empty carton was my table hockey. It was a huge, awesome game that had cost five hundred dollars. It even had a hard clear dome on top! That was my favorite toy, even if I didn't have anyone to play it with. Maybe my cousins would like to play. The only problem was that it was bigger than the carton. If I took that, then there'd be room for hardly anything else, not even my CD player and speakers. My cousins had to have a CD player, so maybe I'd just bring my forty favorite music CD's and then put the hockey game on top.

I got up and tip-toed barefoot through all the toys on the floor, over to my music case. I began to flip through my CD's. It would be a long process to decide which to take. I picked up the first CD. Dinosaur Rock. Kid stuff. No way. I tossed it on the floor, creating a 'No Way' pile. Next was Sunset Rap. Yes. Definitely. Luckily my mom couldn't understand the words on that CD or she'd never let me listen. Best of the Eagles? That was my father's favorite. Dad did have okay taste in music. I'd keep it. I put it on top of Sunset Rap. I looked at the case full of CD's. It would be a very long process.

Going through my CD's did take a long time. Trying to go to sleep that night took even longer. But sleep finally did arrive, and shortly after waking up the next morning it was time to leave.

"Jason, we need to go!" Mom called from the bottom of the stairs.

"In a minute," I yelled back. I just sat on my bed, unable to believe that this would be the last time I would ever be in this room. The toys and clothes I wasn't taking were scattered everywhere. My mother had said that some guys would come by later and put everything into boxes and then send them to storage. My old stuffed animals looked sad at being left behind. Monkey-Eat-A-Spice had that same sewed-on, red-threaded grin that he always had, but he didn't look happy today. That stuffed monkey was old and gray with almost no hair left, but he had been my favorite when I was little. More than anything I had wanted to include him in one of those three cartons. But my cousins would think that I was a baby if I brought a stuffed animal. So Monkey-Eat-A-Spice was sentenced to storage. STORAGE. I shuddered. It sounded like prison. It would be for Monkey-Eat-A-Spice.

"Jason!" Mom yelled one more time.

Why was it so hard to leave? I didn't have too many happy memories in this house. The few times other kids had come over, they thought it was a great house with lots of fun toys.

I hardly knew any kids in my town. I went to a private school which was a 40 minute drive away, and so none of the kids at my school lived near me. And my hockey team took kids from my town and a few others. Nearly all the other kids lived in those other towns. Plus there weren't many other houses nearby which might have kids. My mother liked to say we lived in an 'exclusive' neighborhood. That meant expensive. It also meant that the houses were far apart and hardly any other kids were around.

I felt sad and scared. It felt like I was leaving my father for good. My father had never had much time to do things with me, but he was still my dad. And I was nervous about moving in with my cousins. I liked the idea of other kids to play with, but those kids scared me. I always felt like a dork around them. They seemed cool, and I never knew quite how to act with them. I was never sure whether they were kidding with me or being mean. It was hard deciding if I should laugh *with* them or get mad *at* them.

"Jason!" I heard my mother climbing the stairs this time when she called.

I hopped from my bed and ran to my bedroom doorway. "I'm leaving right now," I said, giving my room one last look-over. I spotted the small framed picture of my mother, my father and me on top of my dresser. We were sitting on a sleigh at Santa's Village, and I looked about four years old at the time. I barely remembered Santa's Village, but I must have had fun by the way everyone was smiling. I sprinted over to the dresser, grabbed the picture and wrapped it in the jacket I was holding, and ran out of the room without looking back.

"Come on, Jason. There's nothing left for you to pack. What have you been doing?"

"Just looking around, Mom."

My mother looked at me with sad eyes. She leaned over and half hugged me. I wasn't sure if I was supposed to hug back, and so I just stood there. Mom quickly let go, looked away and walked downstairs. I followed her down and out the front door.

"Good-bye, house," I said quietly.

"Huh?" my mother asked.

"Nothing."

We walked across the front lawn to our car which was parked at the end of the driveway. My three cartons were on the back seat with my things piled so high that my hockey game even touched the roof of the car! My mother's stuff was in the trunk. Mom opened her front door and sat down in the driver's seat. I opened the passenger door and sat down, put my folded jacket on my lap and reached for my seat belt. We both slammed our car doors at the same time.

"What's that in your jacket, Jason?"

"Nothing."

"What do you mean *nothing*. You have your three carton's worth of stuff. Grabbing something extra?"

I didn't say anything.

"Let me see that 'nothing' in your jacket. What was so important that you had to keep me waiting?"

I reached in my folded jacket and grabbed the small framed photograph of the three of us at Santa's Village. I handed it to her. She held it and just stared at it for a minute. I couldn't tell if she was mad at me or what. Then I noticed a big tear streaming down her cheek. It rolled right off her chin and even dripped a ways down her blue wind-breaker. Her eyes didn't leave that picture. Finally she just handed it back, wiped the trail of tear from her face with the back of her hand, and started the car. I turned around for one last glimpse of my house, the only house I had ever known. Mom's eyes never wavered from the front of the car. In seconds, our house was out of sight. Maybe forever.

Chapter 4

ENTERING GLENVILLE. The sign I'd been waiting for! I couldn't believe my eyes. We were finally there. I had never sat in a car for so long. From our house we had driven for about six hours, stayed over in a tiny inn, and then driven for almost another full day! But we were there. Glenville was one of the most northern towns in Maine. In fact it was one of the most northern places in the whole country, not counting Alaska! I had spent much of the trip studying our road map, charting our progress. Glenville was practically in Canada. I knew that most of the great hockey players came from Canada, and I grew hopeful about the prospects of hockey in this distant region.

My mom drove slowly through what must have been the town center. There were a few small shops: Cye's Diner, Doucette's Hardware, Chasse's Grocery, Dubay's Ice Cream. Underneath DuBay's Ice Cream the sign said *La Glace*.

"What's *La Glace*?" I asked my mother.

"Huh?"

"*La Glace*, like it says over there on that sign."

My mother slowed down and strained to read the sign. "Probably ice cream. It's French, I think."

"Why do they have signs in French?"

"Lots of French Canadians up here. That's what language they used to speak. Some of them still do, I guess."

The shops were all old-fashioned and kind of neat looking. Each had its own distinctive look. There were no stores I knew like CVS or McDonald's. Almost all the stores had a person's name on the sign, probably the owner's. A huge white church topped by an enormous steeple towered above all the other buildings in the center of town.

My mother leaned forward and glanced down at the hand-written directions resting on the dashboard. "We turn right, here at the church, I think, and then straight for three miles. Or is it right at the next road?"

Two older men were standing chin to chin in front of the church, engaged in an intense conversation or argument. My mother pulled to the side of the road and leaned over me to speak out my open window to them.

"Do you know if the Reeses live down this street?" she asked.

"*Je ne parle pas anglais*," one of the men said, and the other man nodded his head vigorously.

"REESE," my mother enunciated slowly and loudly.

"Ah! Reese!" the other man said excitedly, making a large, encircling motion with his arms, as if to hug a tree trunk.

"Yes!" my mother said, nodding.

The man pointed down the road that my mother had thought they lived on. At the same time his mouth fired a barrage of words that meant nothing to me.

"Thank you, *merci*," my mother said nodding, and we turned and drove off. The town center ended abruptly. Suddenly we were again driving through wide open land. I knew that most of the fields were potato fields up here. We passed an occasional house, many with a religious statue in front, and most with a barn somewhere behind. Then my mother slowed down the car, pulled left into a driveway and came to a stop.

"They're here!" a dirty-faced little girl yelled flashing an ear-to-ear grin. She turned around and scampered wildly across the lawn, up the front steps and into the house.

The house. It looked a lot smaller than I remembered it. In fact it seemed much smaller than my own house, and only three of us had lived there! This was a pretty plain house with white paint that was gray in some spots. Dark green shutters surrounded each window. A massive oak tree towered over the house, shielding it like an umbrella. My eyes were drawn to what looked like the weathered remains of an old tree house at the giant "V" in the lower part of the trunk. The white house and the oak sat alone in the middle of a field, and behind that was the barn, and around the barn were more fields. Potato fields, I assumed.

Aunt Susan came bounding out of the house. Actually it was more like bouncing. Aunt Susan was a very large and round woman in every way. She had a round red face below her round bush of wiry reddish-gray hair, and her body was so round that it looked like it could roll. She looked nothing at all like any of my parents' friends or like the parents of the other kids at Charter Hall School.

With each step her face grew redder, and by the time she reached the car she was so out of breath that she couldn't say a word. But she didn't have to. Her friendly, radiant eyes and open arms said it all. And for a moment, I wasn't so nervous about coming here.

"Susan," my mother politely said as she got out of the car and cautiously stepped into Aunt Susan's wide arms. Aunt Susan didn't appear to notice the awkward stiffness of my mother's body as she nearly lifted my mom off the ground. Aunt Susan seemed to hold her up in the air forever when my eyes at last met my aunt's. My mother practically fell to the ground as my aunt let her go. Aunt Susan rounded the car to greet me.

"Jason, dearie," were her first words as she reached for the door handle. She flinched for a second when the door wouldn't budge. It was locked. My mother always made me ride with the doors locked in case we went through a bad neighborhood. I quickly pressed the electric lock release, and my aunt opened the door and leaned into the car and smothered me with a hug.

"You're looking more like my brother than ever," she whispered, giving me an extra squeeze. When she finally released me and wriggled her way back out of the car, I noticed that her eyes were watery.

"Aren't you going to say anything to your aunt?" she belted out. "Like maybe, 'hello auntie' or 'nice to see you' or 'you're fatter than the last time I saw you?' I am, you know," she laughed, looking at my mother.

"Hi, Aunt Susan," I finally said.

"Well, get outta the car and let me see how tall you've gotten."

I stepped out and stood awkwardly, feeling like I was being inspected. My aunt cocked her head slightly to one side and hummed while she walked in a circle completely around me. Her eyes darted up and down my body the whole time. I felt like the slaves must have felt when they were being sold. There was a picture of a slave auction in my illustrated book about Abraham Lincoln. That image had always haunted and fascinated me.

"His father's son, I do declare," my aunt muttered.

I then noticed the dirty-faced little girl's eyes peeking out from behind my aunt's massive body. Aunt Susan noticed our eyes connect and declared, "How rude of me! Why you probably don't even remember your cousin here. She's just three years old. She wasn't even walking when you were here last. Young boys don't notice nothing that's not old enough to play a little baseball."

"I don't play baseball," I said.

"Why, heavens, that can't be! Your mother is always writing about your sports in her Christmas cards we get each year."

"Hockey, Aunt Susan. I play hockey."

"Hockey, baseball, what's the difference? This little one couldn't play neither when you last saw her, ay-yuh."

Susan reached behind her and yanked at the little girl, practically picking her up by the sleeve of her well worn brown dress. "This here is your cousin Jeannie. Jeannie, this is Jason."

Jeannie giggled and skittered again behind her mother.

"She's a bit shy with strangers at first. It won't last, though. You'll probably wish it would." She gave a short, quick laugh at her cleverness.

By now, three more kids ranging in age from about seven to fourteen stood behind Aunt Susan. I remembered them. The two older boys smiled mischievously at me. Billy was the oldest, then George, and the younger girl was Sally. I was trying to figure out which two Reese children were still missing when Aunt Susan barked, "Don't just stand there like clods, help your family unpack!"

Billy, the fourteen year-old, was tall and thin and had a bony face with dark, hard eyes. George, who was twelve, was much heavier than Billy and almost as tall. He was probably stronger than Billy, but his rounder face gave him a softness that reminded me of Aunt Susan and so he scared me less. I eyed my two older cousins suspiciously as they each grabbed a carton or bag from the car and hauled our stuff toward the house.

Chapter 5

"BOYS, PLEASE SHOW YOUR cousin where he'll be sleeping and both of you guys help him haul his gear up," Aunt Susan said to Billy and George. "And Sally, why don't you heat up some water for tea for your Aunt Ellen?"

"That way," Billy said to me, nodding in the direction of the stairs.

I quickly took in the surrounding rooms. They were surprisingly empty for a family with so many kids. In the living room I noticed one small TV with two couches and an old green stuffed chair facing it. There was one closed wooden cabinet. That probably contained their music system.

"Which of these are yours, Jason?" Aunt Susan asked.

"These are," I answered, pointing to my three cartons.

"Billy, grab one! You too, George!" my aunt ordered, eyeing my mother and shaking her head as mothers often do.

My cousins each grabbed a carton while I picked up the third. Billy led the way up the stairs, I followed, and George trudged behind. I noticed George peeking in one carton to see what I had. At that second, I was relieved that I had decided not to bring along my stuffed animals.

At the second floor, George walked the length of the upstairs hallway, the thick pine floorboards creaking with every step. I peeked into the other bedrooms as I passed them and didn't see any other TV's. With eight people in the family, they couldn't have just one TV! At home, my mother, my father and I each had our own television and VCR so we could each watch our own things.

"In here," George said humorlessly. He stepped into a large bedroom and turned around to face me, the smile now erased from his face. I liked his smiling face better, even if it did have a little of the devil in it.

There were three beds inside, bunk beds along the far wall and a single bed below the window on the left side of the room.

"You sleep there," Billy grunted, pointing to the lower bunk.

"You have an extra bed for me?"

"No, dork. That used to be George's bed," Billy said.

"Where's George going to sleep?"

"Right above you," George spoke up, those mischievous grins appearing once again on the faces of my cousins.

"And who used to sleep there?"

"I did," Billy stated bluntly, the grin gone again.

"Who sleeps there?" I asked, pointing to the single bed.

"Henry," Billy answered. That's right! Henry! He must be nine. He was the one closest to my age.

"What about you, Billy?" I asked my oldest cousin.

There was no humor in fourteen year-old Billy's face when he growled through clenched teeth, "I'm moving in with my sister Jeannie while you're here."

A deafening silence filled the room.

I shuddered, and stuttered, "I..I.. don't m..m..mind sleeping on the floor, you know, like on top of a sleeping bag."

"That's what I said to my mother," Billy grumbled, "but she thought four in a room was too much. She said we'd never get enough sleep. I told her *we* would get plenty of sleep."

I didn't like the way he said 'we.'

"Why don't I sleep with Jeannie. I don't m..m..mind, really," I volunteered.

"We tried that, too," twelve year-old George spoke up. "But my mother thought that it would be a good idea for you to be with the cousins closest to your age."

"I'll tell her that I want to sleep with Jeannie." I said, and I meant it!

"My mom said that if you said that to her, she'd know it came from us. And if that happened, we'd be in *big* trouble. And when my mother says big trouble, she means it."

I could believe that.

By now, George was busily rummaging through a carton of my things.

"Neat hockey game," George said, lifting it out of the carton and then sifting through what remained. "Hey, look at this," he said to his older brother. George tossed The Best of the Eagles CD to Billy.

"What are you gonna do with this?" Billy sneered.

"Listen to it," I answered meekly.

"On what?" Billy asked.

"A CD player."

"Did you bring one?" big George asked.

"There wasn't room in my cartons. I thought that I could listen on yours."

My two older cousins howled in laughter.

".. that is, when you're not listening to your music," I finished.

"Who do we look like, the freaking Rockefellers?" Billy taunted. "You think we own a CD player?"

Billy removed the Eagles compact disk from the case. He flung it to George. "Make's a pretty good frisbee, though."

Luckily George caught it.

"Please give it back," I pleaded.

"Rich boy, are you trying to tell my brother what to do?" Billy demanded.

"No, I was just asking," I whimpered.

"Rule number one, in this house, you do *not* tell us what to do. This is our house and not yours. I don't care what my mother says. Rule number two, you do not go tattle like you always did three years ago. And rule number three, you do not *ask* us to do anything. If you do, you might get what you ask for. George, give him back his CD." My wiry cousin nodded to his younger brother, making a flicking wrist motion to him.

George flung the CD like a frisbee right to me. It wasn't the hardest throw in the world, but it wasn't a soft, easy one either. I reached for the flying disk with my left hand and bobbled it. I held on, falling to the floor, but scraped the disk on the rough floorboards while trying to break my fall.

For a second, I thought that I detected a trace of sympathy on George's round face, but he quickly hid any concern with a shrug of his shoulders and a 'so what' expression.

"Better stick to hockey. You'll never make it as a baseball player," Billy snickered.

I looked at the CD in my hand. Three gashes ran the length of the disk. That was The Best of the Eagles, my father's favorite! It was ruined! I felt wetness well up around my eyes but used all of my will power to force the tears to stay put. I looked up at my cousins. It was going to be much worse than I thought.

Chapter 6

I LAY MOTIONLESS ON my new bed, staring at the rusted springs of the bunk bed above me. My eyes tried to follow the path of a single coil as it spiraled upward. I kept messing up, repeating the same loop. I knew that I should be unpacking my things, but I was too depressed to do anything but just lie there. My two older cousins had run off to play, and they hadn't even invited me to go along. Not that I wanted to play with those guys. But it would have been nice to be asked.

Suddenly, into the bedroom walked another cousin, this time a boy about my own age. I knew he was Henry.

"Hi," Henry said shyly. Henry was skinny with brown hair combed straight to his forehead, almost covering his eyes. He looked down when he spoke.

"Hi," I answered.

Henry just stood there, not saying a word or even moving. I didn't know what to say. I remembered Henry as being less scary than his older brothers. I felt funny saying nothing but didn't want to say anything dumb.

"I'm Jason," I said, finally breaking the painful silence.

"I know. I'm Henry."

"I know. I remember you."

"You do?" Henry asked.

"Yeah. We went sledding together down some neat hill. I didn't have a sled with me, so you shared yours. Remember?"

"Yeah, that was fun. That was when you came here during February vacation. You said that you were going to come and visit every winter. But you didn't come that next winter or even last year. Why not?"

I paused to think.

"I know why," I said. "My hockey. We have lots of games over vacation. Three years ago I was only on an in-house team. But the last two years I played for a travel team, and this year I play for a travel team and a select team. At least I did before I had to come here. And this February I'm going on the Canadian Hockey Tour with a US all-star team."

"But didn't you want to go sledding with me again?"

"Yeah, but the other kids on my team would be mad if I missed some games, especially tournament games which we usually have over vacations. Plus, I don't want my teams to lose, and they probably would without me."

"Wow, you must be really good at hockey," Henry said.

"Yeah, I am," I said, beaming. "Do you ever play hockey?"

"A little. It depends on the weather. Sometimes it isn't cold enough for ice. And sometimes there's too much snow on the pond."

"Pond?" I spit out.

"Yeah, why?"

"I've never skated on a pond. Don't you guys have rinks?"

"There's one in St. Claire, I think. But that's about fifty miles away. So we skate on the pond. It's fun!"

"I heard that pond ice will wreck your skates. Is that true?"

"I don't think so," Henry said. "My skates still work."

"But how often do have them sharpened?"

"Huh?"

"Sharpened. My friend Clay sometimes skates with his family on pond ice, but his dad makes him get his skates sharpened right afterwards, before he can go on the rink again."

"Gee," Henry sighed, shaking his head, "my dad files them once a year, at the start of the season. That's all."

"God, they must be dull as bricks!" I scoffed.

Henry looked down, ashamed.

I saw Henry's look of embarrassment and sensed that I had said something wrong but wasn't sure exactly what. I had just told the truth. Everyone knows that you should get your skates professionally sharpened for every six hours of skating, and more often if the ice is bad.

There were more moments of awkward quiet. Finally, I broke the silence.

"Henry, why do your brothers hate me?"

"What do you mean?"

I went on and explained how meanly they had treated me. "Billy especially," I said. "He seems really bad."

"He's not that bad, Jason," Henry said in a hushed voice. "He's just kind of mad that he's being kicked out of his bedroom. That's all."

"Kind of mad? He practically threatened to kill me, or worse, keep me alive and torture me! He really scares me."

For the first time, Henry looked me right in the eye.

"He scares me too, sometimes, but he doesn't really hurt anyone, not badly. He smacks me and pushes me and plays tricks on me. He really loves to scare me. But he's just messing around."

"He wasn't messing around with me, Henry."

"Well, he does bad stuff to me a lot, but he does a lot of good things too. Last year, Danny McGurty was picking on me at school, and Billy threatened to beat him up. Danny said that he wasn't afraid, that he had a big brother Derrick. Billy gave Derrick a licking later that day, and Danny has been nice to me ever since."

"Oh, Billy beats kids up. That makes me feel much better," I said sarcastically. "What if he decides to beat me up?"

"He never would."

"Why not?"

"My mom would kill him. She threatened to kill any one of us if we were mean to you. And my father would probably put the belt to him. He does that when mom gets really mad."

"Really whip you? Your dad sounds pretty mean!"

"No, he's great. He only does it if we do something really bad. And if he didn't whip us, my mom would probably kill us. He's protecting us. That's what Alice says anyway."

"Alice?"

"My older sister. She's thirteen. You must remember her."

I thought hard. I did recall a girl with long brown hair who was older than me. That must have been Alice. I didn't remember anything else about her, though.

"But Billy can be nice too. Last year, when my bike got run over by a tractor and my mom and dad couldn't afford to get me a new one, Billy lent me ten dollars from his potato money to buy Jake Dubay's old bike. And he must have spent two days fixing it up so I could ride it. He can be mean, but he also does lots of good things like that too. Anyway, what've you got in those boxes?"

"My things. My mother told me that I could only take three cartons full of stuff."

"How much stuff do you have?"

"Hmm. Let's see... I have chests and shelves full of toys, and that doesn't count the stuff my mother put up in the attic. Then there's sports equipment and clothes. I bet I could fill this room pretty much top to bottom with my things," I said proudly.

"Billy says that you're rich. I guess you are."

"I never thought about it, really. Most kids I know have about the same amount of stuff, I think."

"Billy says that you're a spoiled brat. Rich and spoiled."

"I am not!" I snapped back. But the remark was like a knife stabbing me in the chest. I didn't know why, but those words really hurt.

Henry just stood in front of me innocently. Henry wasn't accusing me of anything. He was just passing along the words of his brother. I felt bad about yelling at Henry.

"Let me show you my things," I said in a warmer, conciliatory tone.

Henry smiled.

I got up and moved past the opened box with the CD's in it. I opened the next carton, saying, "This is my favorite box. Super Custom 404's!"

I handed the practically new skates to Henry. Henry's eyes opened as wide as hockey pucks. His mouth dropped. He ran his finger cautiously along the shiny blade embedded in hard white plastic.

"Be careful! Those were just sharpened. You can cut yourself easily on that blade. I saw a picture once in a hockey book where a guy skated over another player and cut his throat. Blood spurted everywhere."

"Gross!"

"Yeah. It was really awesome. It was a color picture and everything."

Henry glanced down at his finger, making sure it was okay.

"And these are my hockey pants. Suprema 2000. The best. I could get hit by a Zamboni with these on and probably not get hurt," I laughed.

Henry laughed too. Then he stopped laughing and asked, "What's a Zamboni?"

"You don't know what a Zamboni is?" I asked incredulously.

Again, Henry looked embarrassed, when in barged Billy and George.

"What have we here?" Billy asked, walking straight to the box of hockey equipment. "Shin pads? Ain't rolled up newspaper good enough for the city boy?"

I shrank back to the bed.

"And look at these gloves!" Billy held up my new black leather gloves with tri-flex thumbs.

"And what are these?" Billy added, pulling out the tattered pair of maroon hockey socks, with more holes than wool. He threw them over to George.

"George, you have better socks than these! And to think we thought he was a rich kid. We must have been wrong! Let me see those."

George tossed them back to Billy.

"Wait! Those are my first -"

"I been needing a fresh rag to polish my bike," Billy interrupted me, smiling that creepy smile again. "These'll do. Let's go, George."

My first hockey socks! The ones I wore from when I was three! He couldn't take them! But I said nothing as my older cousins left the bedroom.

"Hey, Jason, this looks cool!" Henry said, pointing to the domed table hockey game laying on the floor. "Want to play?"

"Sure," I said.

Chapter 7

"NO SCHOOL TODAY," Big John announced loudly as he entered the bedroom. "We're going *au large.*" Big John was my Uncle John, but everyone called him Big John, even his own kids sometimes. I could see why. He was huge! He reminded me of Paul Bunyan but older. You could hardly see any of his rough dark skin between his thick grayish-white hair and his bushy beard.

"Hooray!" Henry squealed from his bed.

I felt torn. I had been scared about starting a new school and meeting a new teacher, but I had also been excited about meeting other kids my own age. And I had looked forward to getting away from George and Billy.

They had been really mean on Saturday, the day we arrived. Billy especially. On Sunday, though, the only thing Billy did was try to make me laugh in church, but I was too nervous to laugh. It was a Catholic Church, and I had never been to one before. There was a picture in the colored glass of a guy shot up full of arrows. It was kind of cool, but it also scared me. Henry told me that it was a stained glass window and that the guy was a famous saint. We never used to go to church, but I had heard from friends that it was boring. With saints like that, maybe it wouldn't be so bad.

Big John turned to leave. "How come we have no school?" I asked my burly uncle before he left. It couldn't be a snow day, not in the first week of October.

"It's the freeze that's coming. They say that the temp's dropping into the teens tomorrow night."

Freeze? Ice? Hockey! I prayed that this might mean skating!

"Yeah!" I exploded, pouncing out of bed sending covers flying.

"Don't get so excited, cuz," George said sleepily after Big John left the room. At least he didn't call me rich boy, like he does when Billy's around, I thought.

"He said we're going *au large*," George continued ominously.

The tone of George's voice made me nervous.

"What's that?" I asked.

"We're going to the fields. Potato fields."

"Potatoes?" I didn't understand.

"The harvester broke down last week. The crop was supposed to be done by Friday. We want to get them picked before the freeze, but the harvester won't be fixed for another week. That means we do it by hand, and when that happens, everyone works."

"The harvester is always breaking down," complained Henry.

"It's a piece of junk, that's why," George said.

"Why don't you buy a new one?" I asked innocently.

"Huh! Billy is right. You are a rich kid who doesn't know nothing."

"What did I say?" I asked, looking toward Henry.

"Do you know how expensive a harvester is? Even an old used one costs more than we can afford to pay..." Henry began.

"We don't have much money, if you haven't figured that out by now, genius," George interrupted. "And wait until you harvest potatoes by hand. You'll know what real work is!"

"What do we do? Is it hard?" I asked Henry.

"No, it's easy. You just follow a tractor and pick potatoes up and put them in a basket, and then dump the potatoes into these big barrels. It's kind of fun!"

"Fun!" George blurted. "You've never had to pick for real, Henry."

"I've worked when the harvester's broken before. And I helped Timmy Doucette pick last year," Henry said.

"Right. You probably picked for a half an hour, then got bored and went inside to watch TV. And Dad never expected you to really work when you picked here. He just let you out there to keep you out of Mom's hair. He'll make you work now, though. He killed me when I was nine. Try picking for ten hours, with barely a break. And try it when you have to get it done fast 'cause there's a frost coming. You've never done that."

"Boys!" Big John's voice boomed from downstairs. "*Allons-y! On y va!*"

I didn't need to know French to figure out that he had said something like 'Get off your butts and move.' Henry and George jumped into their clothes and ran downstairs. I dressed a little more slowly and followed a minute later. I could smell something delicious coming from the kitchen. I hadn't eaten much since coming to the Reeses. I'd been too nervous to be very hungry. But at this second, I realized that I was starved. I let my nose lead me to the kitchen.

When I entered, the whole Reese family was already seated, crowded around the rough wooden table. Everyone except Susan. She was leaning over Big John, scraping pancakes off a heavy black cast iron pan, and dropping them onto his plate.

"Morning," Big John greeted me. "All set to find out the meaning of real work?" His fork looked tiny in his large callused hand, and I felt intimidated, but when I looked into his friendly eyes I was less scared.

"I guess," I answered.

I looked around the table and asked, "Where's my mom?"

"Sleeping," Aunt Susan said without breaking her rhythm as she continued serving the breakfast. "Guess she needs her beauty sleep. And you, young man, need to fill that belly of yours. It's a long time until lunch."

"I don't usually eat much breakfast, Aunt Susan," I said, though those pancakes did smell pretty good and I was hungry. Aunt Susan put a plate in front of me and slid two thick brown pancakes off the pan and onto my plate.

"They're *ployes*. Think of them as fuel," she said, "to keep your engine running. You're gonna need it, trust me."

In one smooth motion, Aunt Susan managed to slap a swab of butter on my pancake-like patties and pour maple syrup on top. I grasped my fork, cut a piece with lots of syrup on it and lifted it into my mouth. Incredible! I had never tasted anything so good in my whole life.

"These are awesome! What did you say they were called?" I asked with my mouth full.

"*Ployes*. They're buckwheat," Sally said. "And we grew the buckwheat."

"Buckwheat," little Jeannie repeated.

"It's real Acadian food," Aunt Susan said. "Fuel for your grandfather when he harvested. Fuel for his father, and his father before him."

"And this syrup is delicious! What brand is it?" I asked.

Everyone at the table laughed.

"Mother nature's brand," Aunt Susan said.

"Mother's Nature," Jeannie tried to repeat.

"Never heard of it," I said.

Everyone laughed again.

"Course not," Billy said. " 'Cause there's no such thing. She's saying it's real maple syrup, from trees, not store bought."

"From *your* trees?"

"Yup," Henry said. "And I help with it."

"Eat up there, Jason," Big John said. "We're going *au large* soon."

I shoveled the delicious pancakes into my mouth, watching hearty George finish his second heaping plateful. Henry caught me looking at George and said, "Nobody packs it away like George. He won the 12-and-under *ployes*-eating contest last year at the Acadian festival."

"What's the Acadian Festival?" I asked.

"Big festival every June. Kind of like a family reunion for Acadian people like us. We get folk coming from as far as Cajun country down in Louisiana. Distant family. Hundreds of relatives come."

"It's awesome," Henry said. "They have great barbecues every day."

"And dances," Alice said.

"I like the talent show best," Sally said. "Last year me and Alice won a second place prize for reciting part of *Evangeline*."

"That's a poem by Henry Wadsworth Longfellow," Alice explained. "It's about Acadians, like us, who were sent away from here in the 1700's because they spoke French, and they wouldn't sign a loyalty oath to the English. Some of them journeyed back here. Others just tried to find their loved ones. It's about one of those trips."

"*Thus dwelt together in love these simple Acadian farmers,*" Sally recited from memory.

"*Dwelt in the love of God and of man,*" Alice continued. "*Alike were they free from fear, that reigns with the tyrant, and envy, the vice of the republics.*"

Sally picked it up. "*Neither locks had they to their doors, nor bars to their windows, but their dwellings were open as day and the hearts of the owners.*"

"*There the richest was poor and the poor lived in abundance,*" Alice finished.

"And Big John played the part of Evangeline's father, Benedict," Sally said.

"*Hearty and hale was he, an oak that is covered with snowflakes. White as the snow were his locks, and his cheeks were as brown as the oak leaves,*" quoted Alice, pointing to Big John and laughing.

"Except Dad's hair and beard aren't completely white yet so we used chalk dust," Sally said. "We memorized four pages of the poem! The whole thing was too long, about 100 pages. And then we just told people how it ended. It was sad. There were lots of other neat acts, too, at the festival."

"I like the trees best," Jeannie said, clapping her hands.

"Trees get planted as monuments," Aunt Susan explained, "to honor families, families whose roots are in this land."

"How come we never came?" I asked. "We're relatives."

"You did once," Aunt Susan said. "But you were just a baby. Every year since then, your dad's always been too busy with his job."

"I never even knew about it," I said, feeling a little hurt, as I washed down my last bite of *ployes* with a tall glass of orange juice.

"Mm. This orange juice is delicious. Do you grow your own oranges too?"

"No. Too cold up here for that," Aunt Susan answered. "We grow a lot of things but not oranges."

Big John disappeared for a few minutes and returned with a large cardboard box full of brown gloves and jackets.

"*Les premiers arrivés, seront les premiers servis,*" he announced, as the four oldest Reese children all jumped from the table and dove for the carton. His eye then caught mine and he said quietly, "First come, first served."

"I had that pair!" Henry yelled.

"I had it first," George said.

"Give it back!" Henry whined.

"*Taisez-vous*! Hush!" Big John boomed. "Give that pair of gloves to Jason. Find some others for yourselves."

George instantly handed over the gloves to me. They were stiff and dirty. I was pretty sure that they were leather, but they felt more like cardboard.

"Billy honey, give your cousin a jacket that fits him," Aunt Susan said.

Billy grabbed the jacket on top and tossed it to me.

"Can I go too?" Sally asked.

Big John and Aunt Susan just looked at each other.

"The boys used to pick when they were seven. They started when they were six!" Sally said.

"Sally, they have a lot of work. You'll only get in the way. Besides, you'll have a lot more fun at school."

"Mom, I'll watch out for her," Alice volunteered. "I started when I was seven. She won't get in the way."

"All right with me so long as you do your share, Alice," Big John said to his thirteen year-old daughter. "I need you too much out there to have you just baby-sitting."

"Don't worry, Dad," Alice assured her father.

Sally looked to her mother for final approval.

"Okay," Aunt Susan said.

"*Allons-y*," Big John said, leading a trail of Reese kids out the door. I followed.

Billy led the way to the potato fields while Big John headed to the barn to get the tractor. I breathed deeply. The crisp Maine air chilled my face but felt good in my lungs. The recently risen sun was still low in the sky and hadn't yet burned off the dew from the weedy field we were traipsing through. I heard the roar of the tractor engine as Big John started it, and minutes later it was steaming over one field heading toward the potatoes.

"Here are your baskets," my uncle said, stepping down from the tractor and handing each of us a strong woven basket. "When you fill it up, mark a barrel and dump your basket in it. Five dollars a barrel."

I looked at a barrel. It would take a lot of potatoes to fill one of those barrels! And only five bucks. Five bucks was nothing. That's less then than two skate sharpenings! Five bucks was what my mother paid for a half hour of power skating drills. But something told me to keep my mouth shut and just do the work. I had never worked before. I had never earned my own money. Whenever I wanted anything, my parents just bought it. Things were different here.

I grabbed my basket. It was old and weathered but seemed strong. I began to get eager about the job that lay ahead. Earning my own money started to feel exciting. Maybe I could even earn enough to join a hockey team! My mother was going to make some calls today about youth hockey teams up here. It had only been a few days since I had skated in my last game, but it seemed like forever. I missed the ice. It was like part of me was not alive when I couldn't skate.

"Let's go!" George said as Big John began to plow the first row. The plow turned over the top layer of soil, and there, half buried in dirt and rocks, were potatoes just waiting to be picked up.

"George and I will do these first two rows," Billy stated. "Alice! You, Henry, Sally and Jason can do the next row."

Alice and Henry nodded okay, and I followed them to the start of the next row where we waited for Big John to return. I was relieved to get a few minutes to watch Billy and George pick first. The two older boys leaned over and quickly grabbed into the dirt at anything round. Potatoes went into their baskets and rocks were tossed aside. But I could barely see the two boys do their job through the thick brown cloud of dust kicked up by the tractor.

Big John got to the end of the row and began to return. The roar of the engine got louder as the cloud of dust approached.

"It's our turn in a second," Alice announced.

Big John got to the three children and turned the tractor around to plow the next row.

"Stay back!" Alice commanded with the authority of an adult, firmly putting a hand on Sally's shoulder.

The tractor moved on.

"Okay," Alice yelled above the roar of the powerful engine.

Alice instantly leaned over and began to grab potatoes and put them into her basket. I did the same. I felt the thrill in my heart as I leaned over and picked up my first potato! It was filthy, but it was a potato! So this is how potatoes were picked. These same potatoes might be in a bag some day in a grocery store. Maine Potatoes. That's what the bag would say. No one would know that I, ten year-old Jason Quinn, had done the picking. I looked through the dust at my cousins. Alice and Henry must have had a dozen potatoes each in their baskets. I leaned down next to my cousins and began to pick up more potatoes. Each few filled up my basket higher and higher. It felt good, like I was getting somewhere. And I was making money. Hockey money! Before my first basket was filled, I began to feel tired. But the excitement of this new job and the thought of making money to be able to play hockey let me forget about my aching body.

I watched Alice's hands move as fast as Mario Lemieux's hands stick-handing a puck. No matter how hard I tried, I could never pick that fast. But it didn't matter. I was having fun.

Chapter 8

FUN... HOW COULD I HAVE thought that picking potatoes would be fun? I could barely move, but I had to get out of bed. I needed to get dressed, eat breakfast, sweep the back hall, which was my morning chore, and get to the bus stop. All in forty-five minutes! It could be worse. I might have to pick potatoes all day again. That would be much worse. Big John had hired some Mic Mac Indians to help out so we kids could go to school. We'd still have to help after school, but that would only be for a couple of hours.

Henry had explained that the Mic Mac Indians were migrant workers who came down from Canada each year during potato harvesting season. Then when they finished their picking they'd move somewhere else, someplace where there was more work to do. They didn't really have a place that was their home. They were sort of like hockey referees, I thought. Always going to where the next job was.

The Mic Macs were supposed to be unbelievably fast workers. Alice had told me that a good Mic Mac could pick a hundred barrels of potatoes a day. No way, I thought. I had only filled six barrels working from eight in the morning until six at night. Thirty bucks, and I had killed myself. I was looking forward to seeing some Mic Macs in action after school. Alice must have exaggerated.

But how could they stand doing it? My back killed from all the leaning over. My knees ached from squatting then standing then squatting then standing. And the dirt. That was the worst part. I didn't know that anyone could ever get so dirty. It got in my eyes, in my ears, down my throat and up my nose. There

44

was still black coming out when I blew my nose before going to bed. My hands had even gotten black, and I'd worn those thick gloves all day! George had complained about the boredom, but I thought that the dirt was the worst part of the job.

"Jason, get up!" Henry said, giving my covers a quick jerk.

"I'm trying," I groaned.

"Yesterday was a little rough, huh?" George said, but not meanly.

"Kinda," I answered shyly.

"You get used to it. Maybe a little boring, but it's not so bad."

I said nothing.

"And yesterday," George continued, "you did all right for your first time."

"Not too bad for a city boy," Billy said, walking into the bedroom. "I didn't think that you'd make it the full day. But you did. You might not have picked any more than eighty year-old Mr. James does, but you stuck it out. What'd you make, about twenty-five bucks?"

"Thirty."

"If you don't drop, you'll make forty today," Billy said.

"But we're going to school today! Aunt Susan said so!"

"That was before Big John talked with her this morning. Seems the Mic Macs got another job and can't help. That leaves just us."

I felt sick. I wanted to throw up. I really didn't know if I could make it through another whole day picking potatoes. And if I couldn't, my cousins would never let me hear the end of it. 'City boy,' 'rich kid.' It would all start again. How was I going to do it?

Footsteps pounded up the stairs outside the bedroom.

"Get up, now!" Aunt Susan hollered. "The school bus leaves in half an hour!"

"But what about the potatoes?" I asked.

"Big John got some Mic Macs to help out. It's school for you guys."

Hadn't she talked with Big John yet? Doesn't she know that the Mic Macs can't make it? I started to say something to my aunt when I noticed the grins on the faces of my older cousins. Billy and George were holding their mouths tightly, swallowing their laughs.

"What's that, Jason?" Aunt Susan asked.

I glanced at Billy. Billy very slightly shook his head 'no.'

"Nothing," I said, getting into my regular clothes.

"No *ploges* today. School days, we just have cereal and toast. It's a lot faster. So let's go!" Aunt Susan said, leaving the room to go back downstairs.

Three year-old Jeannie ran into the room and shouted, "Let's go!" She then giggled and ran out, following her mother.

When Aunt Susan was walking back down the stairs, Billy and George bent over in laughter. I felt like a fool. Why had I believed them! How could they be so mean?

I looked to Henry. Henry wasn't mean, but he was smiling too.

"Henry!" I whined, my eyes pleading for support.

"It was a joke, Jason. Lighten up," Henry said.

Easy for you to say, I thought. They didn't make you look like a jerk.

"And it was pretty funny. You should have seen your face," Henry laughed. Billy and George smiled again.

I wanted to smile as well, but I couldn't. I just scowled at my cousins and stomped out of the bedroom and down to breakfast.

"Good morning, stranger," my mother greeted me at the bottom of the stairs.

"Where were you last night?" I grilled her. After killing myself in the field all day, I had been further upset when my mother was not around and never even got back all evening.

"I had things I had to deal with," my mom said.

"Like finding me a hockey team?" I asked, wide-eyed.

"I'm sorry. I'm afraid that I never got around to that."

"But you promised me that you would yesterday. You promised!"

"Jason, I said that I'd try to do it. I have other things. Pressing matters. I'll find out about hockey soon. I promise."

"Today," I insisted.

"Maybe. Listen, did Aunt Susan tell you that I'd be away for a while? There's business that I need to deal with in Boston. It might be a few weeks until I'm back."

A few weeks! It felt like someone slammed me in the chest. I was stunned but quickly regained my composure. "At least don't forget about the Canadian Tour," was all I said.

From in the kitchen, Aunt Susan's voice rang out, "Jason!" She had a smooth, full voice, as round as the rest of her.

"Coming!"

I sat down at the table in front of a full bowl of corn flakes. I reached for my spoon and shoveled in a mouthful.

Yuch! They didn't taste quite right. They were a little soggy or something. They didn't seem like the ones at home.

"Are these corn flakes?" I quietly asked Henry, who was sitting to my right.

"Sure. Look at the box over there."

Henry pointed to the counter top next to the sink. There sat the hugest box of cereal that I had ever seen. It was an enormous white box that was almost as big as Jeannie! In black letters were the words, 'Toasted Flakes of Corn.'

"Those aren't the kind we get," I said.

"Warehouse Club," Aunt Susan piped in. "This family would starve without that place."

"It's generic cereal," my mother patiently explained, sitting down in the empty chair to my left.

Generic food. Yuch! My mother had never bought generic food. Only name brand foods. Mom had always said they tasted the best. She sure was right.

I noticed Aunt Susan sending a questioning glare toward my mother.

"I told him!" my mother whispered sharply to my aunt.

"I see the bus!" Alice called from the front hall.

"Get going!" my aunt commanded.

"Aunt Susan, can I sweep later?" I asked, getting up from the table.

She nodded yes.

As I raced out the door, I instantly stopped and turned around quickly. "Bye, Mom," I said.

"Good-bye, Jason. Good luck at school."

I wanted to say something else, but I was in a hurry. I was also mad at her for leaving me here alone in what felt like enemy territory. And I was angry that she had not done anything about the hockey yet. But I knew that I would still miss her. I left my mixed emotions at the doorway and raced off for the school bus.

School. A new school, I thought. Nervous and excited, I followed my cousins to the bus. The Reese kids were all sprinting down the sidewalk while the bus waited for them at the corner. As I was running, I glanced up toward the bus and took in a flash of unfamiliar faces. Then, boom!

I was flat on my back. Ow! My butt really hurt! Instantly I was furious at my cousins. George or Billy must have planted something to make me trip. And in front of all these new kids! I glanced up at their gawking faces pressed against the bus windows, and I felt my face burn. I was mortified! And I was so mad! I pushed myself up off the ground and began walking to the bus. My feet slipped a little.

At that moment I looked down on the sidewalk. My cousins hadn't tricked me. It was ice. Ice! I had slipped on a small patch of ice on the sidewalk. Just as I was beginning to feel sorry for myself again, being embarrassed and all in front of these new kids, the word sunk in. *Ice*! I hadn't noticed how cold it was. Ice! Hockey! How cold does it have to be for the ponds to freeze? I forgot all about school for a minute. All I could think of was one thing. Ice.

Chapter 9

"WHO'S THE NEW KID, Henry?" a tall blonde boy asked as if I were not even there.

"Oh, this is my cousin. Carl, this is Jason. He's going to be going to school with us. He's living with us for a while."

Five strange boys stood around me, carefully checking out the stranger in their midst. I looked back at them trying to decide if they were good kids. They all had longer hair than the boys back home, and they looked a little tougher. I was wondering about what made them look tougher. The shortest one, with long black hair, had crooked yellow front teeth and dark, deep eyes. Another kid had brown hair parted in the middle. He had a hard round face and small dirty hands with short stubby fingers. His dark brown eyes glared into mine. I looked away.

"Jason, these are some of the kids in my grade. I'll tell you who they are later. We have to get to class now," Henry said, walking toward the front of the school.

The school was so small, it looked more like a big house. A school house. It wasn't at all like Charter Hall School. My school at home had lots of different buildings, each bigger than Henry's whole school. There was the building for Pre-K through first grade. Then the second and third graders were in a different building. And the fourth, fifth and sixth graders were in the Main Building. Plus there was the Science Building the Arts Building and a gym.

I followed Henry into the school house and around the corner into a large classroom with desks lined in perfect rows. None of the classrooms at Charter Hall had rows. The desks were all in work clusters, and there were a lot fewer desks in each classroom.

"Come here," Henry directed me, leading me to the front of the class. An older woman with reddish brown hair and glasses sat behind the teacher's desk. She was busy marking papers with a colored pencil. I noticed a lot of red marks on the worksheet in front of her. Not a good sign.

"Excuse me, Miss Loder," Henry spoke politely.

The teacher finished writing something, then placed the red pencil down next to the paper and looked up at Henry.

"Yes, Henry?"

"Miss Loder. This is Jason. He's my cousin and he'll be going to school with us for a while."

"So I've heard. Jason Quinn, is that correct?" she asked, looking directly into my eyes.

"Yes."

She put out her hand and smiled. "Well, I'm very pleased to meet you, Jason Quinn. I'll be your new teacher, Miss Loder."

Reaching out, I gently squeezed her hand and let go.

"That's no way to shake a hand, Jason," she whispered to me. "A man in these parts is measured by the strength of his handshake. Try again."

I shook Miss Loder's hand once again, this time squeezing harder.

"That's a little better, Jason, but you want to work on that some more. You don't want to break my hand but let me feel some substance next time. And look me in the eye as well."

I nodded.

"Jason, you may sit in that desk, next to Henry."

Miss Loder pointed to an empty seat in the front row. I walked to it and sat down. All the other children were already seated. I wished that I were sitting more in the back of the class, less under those hawklike eyes of Miss Loder, and more where I could better check out the other kids in class. I turned around to see what my classmates looked like. The eyes of every kid in the class were glued to me, and I quickly turned back to the front. The only impression that I got was that they were big. Really big. It must be all the potatoes they feed them up here.

"Class, please stand for the Pledge of Allegiance," Miss Loder announced, carefully enunciating each word.

The class immediately obeyed and cited in unison, "I pledge allegiance to the flag of the United States of America..."

I had heard this before, but didn't know the words. They never said it at Charter Hall School. But I mumbled and moved my lips a little so that no one would know that I didn't know the words. I felt nervous sweat gather under my arms.

"...with liberty and justice for all," the class finished.

"You may be seated," Miss Loder said.

Phew, I thought, getting into my seat. No one had noticed me faking it.

"And class, we have a new student with us today. His name is Jason Quinn. He's Henry and George's cousin. Jason, would you come up here?"

I felt the stares of twenty-five kids penetrate my skin as I stood and stepped up to Miss Loder.

"Turn around, Jason, and let the class see you. They need to do their looking now so we can get on to other business soon and not be distracted. Excuse their staring, Jason. It's not often we get a new face in this school."

At Charter Hall School, there were three or four new kids in a class each year! And a couple came or left during the year. A parent changing jobs was usually the reason.

I looked toward my new classmates, trying to avoid their direct stares. Then I saw him. In the back row. George! What was he doing in this class? George was two years older than me! George was twelve. Maybe he got kept back, I thought.

"Jason, welcome to Purcell Elementary School. Would you mind telling the class where you are from and a little bit about yourself?"

I moved my lips, but nothing came out.

"Just relax," Miss Loder said in a soothing but professional voice. "Public speaking is a difficult task. We all do a lot of it in this class. I believe that it is an invaluable life skill, and the more you do, the less nervous you get. Just do your best, Jason."

The class waited soundlessly.

I breathed in deeply and exhaled. "My name is Jason Quinn. I come from near Boston. That's a city in Massachusetts."

I stopped. More silence.

"Can you tell us something about yourself?" Miss Loder asked, breaking the silence.

"I play hockey. I played for the Greater Boston Junior Terriers. They're a select Squirt team, one of the best in Massachusetts. I started playing with them last spring. I also play on my town's Squirt I team, and even though I was one of the youngest players last year, I was the second leading goal scorer on the team."

I breathed again, feeling more relaxed now. Talking about hockey was something that I could do easily.

"I've been playing hockey since I was three years old, and I was on a team when I was four. All the other kids on the team were mostly seven, eight or nine years old. I was pretty good on that team, even though I was only on the third line and it was an in-house team. And when the other kids found out how old I was, they couldn't believe it. That year I..."

"Okay," Miss Loder interrupted. "Maybe your classmates would like to know something else about you?"

"Why'd you move here?" a red-headed girl in the middle of the class asked.

"Darlene, raise your hand the next time," Miss Loder corrected her. "Jason?"

"We had to move out of our house," I said, feeling a little embarrassed.

"I heard your old man's a crook, and that's why," a big kid near George said. "And he was so ashamed of his family that he changed his name."

"That's enough!" Miss Loder said sharply. "And Mr. Haskins, I'll speak with you after class."

I wouldn't want to be that kid, I thought.

"Any *other* questions?"

Silence.

"Very well. Thank you, Jason. And welcome once again. You may be seated."

I walked to my seat. As I did, I thought about what that kid had said. Did my father really break the law? My mother had mentioned money problems, but she never said that he was a criminal.

The morning went by quickly. There were lots of activities, like at my old school, but everyone stayed in one class. At one point, Miss Loder separated the fourth, fifth and sixth graders. That's why there were so many big kids, I thought. There was more than one grade in a class! And that explained George. He had just turned twelve, and so he must be in the Sixth Grade.

I was not happy about having George in my class. One reason I had looked forward to school was so that I could get away from George and Billy. Now this. And I worried that George's friends wouldn't be any better. If the Haskins kid was any indication, I was right.

Finally lunch came. I took out the brown bag that Aunt Susan had prepared. Peanut butter and jelly. Just like at home. At least that was the same.

We all ate quietly at our seats, and when Henry finished his lunch and got up, I followed. The schoolyard was a field which was mostly dirt and some weeds. We noticed a gang of kids gathered in the corner.

"Let's see what's going on," Henry said.

We ran to the cluster of kids.

George was grabbing the Haskins boy by the shirt collar.

"Take it back," George ordered.

Haskin's face was turning red, but he fearlessly growled through clenched teeth, "Can't take back what's true."

George pushed him away and threatened, "Later!"

Was George defending me?

"Hey George, was that about me?" I asked, following my older cousin.

"Yeah," George spit out in disgust.

"Thanks," I said.

"Don't thank me," George shot back, turning around and glaring at me. "You're the problem here. You'll get yours later."

Chapter 10

THE ICE WAS STILL FROZEN as I strolled toward the school bus to go home.

"Will anyone play hockey today?" I asked Henry.

"Hey, Guy, anyone playing hockey today?" Henry asked one the bigger kids also heading our way.

"Not on the pond. That needs three or four nights like last night and then maybe some more. But I flooded the fill two nights ago. That might be frozen. We'll check it out."

Hockey! This afternoon!

"Is your cousin as good a puckster as he says he is?" Guy asked Henry. Guy DuBois (pronounced DooBwah) was tall and solidly built. He had that handsome, rugged look of an athlete, the kind you might see on the front of a Wheaties box.

"Don't know. I've never seen him play. But his equipment is pretty awesome."

"Come and play with us, squirt," Guy said to me. "We'll see what you're made of."

"How'd you know I was a Squirt?" I asked him. "I'm pretty big for my age, and a good hockey player, and so most people think I'm a Pee Wee." Pee Wee is the next level after Squirt.

"What are you talking about?" Guy asked, shaking his head. "Just come and play if you want."

"Henry, we can play hockey today! I can't believe it!"

"*We* can't play today, Jason. *We*'re working the fields again. The frost is supposed to get worse tonight. We need to finish."

My stomach instantly turned sickish. There might be hockey and I wouldn't play! I couldn't think of anything worse! I wouldn't have a chance to show these guys how good I was!

56

On the bus, I could think of nothing but hockey. I hated to pick potatoes, but not playing hockey was much worse.

"There's the fill," Henry said, pointing to an open area off the road to our left. There was the ice! It wasn't a very big area, but it was ice! It looked a little bigger than half a hockey rink, maybe wider too. My thoughts dwelled even more on my favorite sport.

When the bus pulled to the side of the road near our house, Henry got up first and I followed. George, Alice and Sally came next. Alice led the way back to the house. She actually seemed to like to pick potatoes! For one thing, she was good at it. She had picked thirty barrels the day before! Maybe if I worked as fast as Alice, I'd like it better. I'd certainly like making all that extra money. I had been impressed with how fast her hands moved. I didn't believe that anyone could work faster. I'd have to see if those Mic Mac Indians picked as quickly as they said.

At the house, the Reese children all went straight to their rooms and got right into their work clothes. Billy was already in the fields working. The junior high got out a little earlier than the elementary school.

"Jason, let's go!" Henry said, interrupting my dream of pucks, sticks and ice. "You're not even dressed! Dad gets real mad if we're late!"

"Okay, I'll be out in a second."

Henry and George went out the bedroom door and ran downstairs to claim their work gloves.

My Super Custom 404's sat on top of the carton at the end of my bed. I could be using those skates. I could be on the ice this afternoon! And then an idea crept into my head. Not a good idea. I tried to sweep it away but I didn't sweep too hard. I looked out the bedroom window and spotted my cousins marching toward the potato field. Henry was walking with George, and Sally was trailing a step behind Alice. I knew that those guys would pick barrels of potatoes. And there were the

Mic Mac Indians. One Mic Mac would pick more in ten minutes than I'd pick all afternoon. They wouldn't miss me. So, I wouldn't get the money, but it wouldn't be much anyway. Suddenly, my idea didn't seem so bad. I would skip potato picking today. I'd play hockey instead!

The ice was about a mile from our house, I thought, but I hadn't paid too much attention on the bus ride. I should be able to walk there in about twenty minutes.

Should I carry my equipment or wear it? It might be pretty heavy to carry my bag. I'd wear most of my stuff and carry my sticks, gloves, skates and helmet. Instantly, my body switched to high gear. I dug into my equipment carton and put on my stuff: cup first, then shin pads, Junior Terrier hockey socks and garter, hockey pants, shoulder pads, elbow pads and jersey. I'd wear my Junior Terrier shirt. It was a game shirt and not supposed to be worn to practice, but I wasn't on the team anymore. It would really impress the other guys.

I threw my skates, gloves and helmet into my hockey bag and grabbed my best two sticks and was off. Aunt Susan was down in the cellar doing the laundry with Jeannie, and so going out of the house was easy. From the front door, I walked to the side of the house and peeked around the corner to the back to see if anyone was looking for me. Everyone was far off on the other side of the potato field, following Big John's tractor.

I trotted awkwardly with my hockey bag and sticks and didn't stop until I was up the street a ways and out of sight of the potato fields. I couldn't believe it! I was actually going to play hockey again!

Even loaded with my equipment and lugging my hockey bag, I was so excited that I moved with an extra hop to my step. It wasn't long, though, before that extra hop disappeared. I used to complain to my mother about having to walk from the house to the car carrying all my hockey gear. This was much tougher.

Soon my pace lessened to a casual walking speed and it wasn't long before it slowed down further. But I walked, and walked, and walked...

The cold wind whipping against my face couldn't stop the sweat from pouring down my forehead. I hadn't brought a watch with me, but I must have been walking for more than an hour! My hockey bag got heavier by the minute, and my strategy of alternating arms to lug it had stopped working long ago. Where was that ice?

Maybe I had taken the wrong road. But I was pretty sure that there was just one road that the bus was on. The ice had to be coming up soon. Had I passed it by? No way. Impossible. I could smell ice.

I heard an engine slow up behind me. I was walking off the road a bit since there was no sidewalk and the massive logging trucks scared me when they whizzed past. I glanced over my shoulder and saw a rusty red pick-up truck pull off the road almost next to me. An older man reached across the front seat and rolled down his window.

"Want a lift?" the man asked in a friendly voice.

"No, thank you," I answered automatically. My parents had taught me to never get into a car with a stranger.

"Where you heading?"

My parents had taught me not to talk to strangers as well. But they also taught me not to be rude. What should I do? I looked again at the driver of the car. He had longish white hair and wore a green and white checked flannel jacket. He didn't look like a bad guy.

"So, where you going?" the old man repeated.

I looked up, not sure what to do. "The fill, where the kids play hockey." The words seemed to come out by themselves.

"You're looking pretty tired there, son. It's another mile or more to the fill. Sure you don't want a lift?"

A mile! The hockey bag instantly grew heavier. By the time I got there, I would be too exhausted to play! They'd never know how good I really was.

"Maybe I *will* go with you," I answered.

The man opened the passenger door and said, "Throw your gear in back and come on in here."

Was this the biggest mistake of my life? I knew that my mother would kill me for doing this. My parents always told me about the bad people who take kids. No, I shouldn't do it.

I was just about to toss my hockey bag into the back of the truck when I stopped.

"Actually, I think I'll walk. Thank you anyway."

"You must be a city boy," the man said. "Where you from?"

"Boston."

The man laughed a full, crackly laugh. "That explains it. If I lived in Boston, I'd never get into a truck with a stranger. Your folks have taught you good! So listen. I know that you need a ride to the fill. My name's Leland McPherson. I been living in these parts for sixty-nine years. Everyone knows me."

"The Reeses know you?" I asked.

"Big John! I've known Big John since he was in diapers. That's a sight, huh? Big John so little he was in diapers! Hah!" He laughed and slapped his knee.

If he knew the Reeses, he must be okay.

"And Susan is quite a woman. A lotta woman, too! They have some clan, ay-yah. How many young-uns are there now, five?"

"Six."

"Whoa!" the man hooted. "I know Billy. He worked for me last summer for the corn harvest. Good boy, that Billy. Can't say I know the others. Six of them now," he chuckled, shaking his head. "Now, you're not a Reese. I might not know their names, but I know a Reese when I see one. I don't recognize you, but I see a little of the family in you still."

"My Dad was Susan's brother."

"Still is, I reckon. You don't stop being a brother when you get older."

"My Dad's dead," I said, realizing that I hadn't thought about him in a long time. None of the Reeses ever mentioned my father. I knew that Aunt Susan had told them not to. She didn't want me to be sad.

"Oh, I'm sorry. Albert, right?"

I was startled.

"I knew your dad. I know everyone in these parts. I'm real sorry he's dead. He was a smart guy, your dad. We all knew that Glenville would never hold a boy like that. I heard he went to some fancy school and really made something of himself, ay-yuh."

I knew that my father had gone to a good college, but that had never seemed special to me. And my dad did have an important job and made a lot of money, but that hadn't seemed unusual either. Mr. McPherson talked like those things made my father really extraordinary. I hoped that Mr. McPherson didn't know about the money problems with my father's business.

"Listen, hop in the back of this truck if it'll make you feel more comfortable and let me give you a lift. That way, if I try to kidnap you, it'll be easier to escape." He winked at me and said, "I'm really not a bad guy."

I was sure that I could trust this man. He knew my dad! Besides, in the back of the truck, I could always scream or jump out. I wouldn't be trapped.

"Okay."

I tossed my bag into the back of the pick-up truck and hopped in there myself. The truck's engine sputtered, then sprang to life, and in two minutes, we slowed down and came to a stop. I threw my bag out of the truck and onto the ground. I hopped over the side of the old truck and jumped down, almost landing on my hockey bag.

"Thanks!" I said.

"Have fun," old Leland McPherson said, then drove off.

I looked toward the ice. There were about fifteen kids there, some playing hockey and another group just skating. I was so excited! Most of the hockey players were older boys, but I knew that I would be one of the best. They hadn't been skating on hockey teams since they were four. They hadn't been coached and been to hockey clinics.

Chapter 11

"HEY, LOOK WHO'S HERE. It's little Wayne Gretzky!" Guy called out across the ice.

I glided over the frozen surface. A few leaves and small sticks were embedded in the top of the ice, and so it was a little bumpy, but not as bad as I had expected. I skated toward the left, crossed over, and then skated toward the right. I followed the weaving pattern across the ice, hoping that everyone was looking at me as I executed my crisp crossovers. Just before I got to Guy I accelerated a little then turned my skates sharply to the left, coming to an instant stop and spraying snow all over Guy's skates.

"It's the puckster," Guy said, ignoring my antic.

"Huh?" I asked.

"Puckster. You know, hockey player."

"What are you wearing all that stuff for?" a kid near Guy asked me. "This is just pond hockey, not the NHL."

I looked at the other kids and it suddenly occurred to me that I was the only one on the ice with any hockey equipment. The other kids had sticks and skates, but no helmets or pads or anything else. At our rink at home, a player can't even get on the ice without full equipment! The first time I ever had a hockey practice, I showed up without a neck guard and I wasn't allowed to play. Just watching that practice from behind the glass was the longest and most painful fifty minutes of my life.

I didn't know what to say so I just shrugged my shoulders. There were about eight boys with sticks at the pond, all around George's or Billy's age. They were surrounding me and gaping at me as if I were an alien or something. Some of them were snickering.

I looked beyond at the girls and the younger boys. They were on the other side of the ice and not all of them had sticks. Clearly, serious hockey was for these older boys only. And I wanted to be part of it. I wanted to be the best player, and then they'd like me.

"Can I play?" I finally asked.

"Yeah. You be on my team," Guy said. "It's you, me, Gary, and Chad." Guy pointed to the kids on our team. I tried hard to remember who they were. It would be tough without uniforms. And I didn't know these guys so they all looked kind of the same to me. I'd figure it out, though, when the game started.

"J.B., you guys can have Ben since we have the kid."

"But then you guys will be short one. Plus you have the little kid."

"If the little puckster is half as good as he says he is, we'll whip your butts," Guy said.

"Let's do it," J.B. said. J.B.'s real name was Jean-Baptiste LeClaire. 'Jean' is French and is pronounced more like 'John,' except with a softer 'J' sound. His family is French-Canadian. George had told me that when Jean was little, the kids in school used to make fun of him for having a girl's name. So he started having people call him J.B. for Jean-Baptiste.

Guy turned to me. "You'd better be as good as you say. I hate to lose, especially to J.B.. Goals are between the boots, no lifts, no going down in front of the net. Okay?"

I looked at the playing surface. At one end, a pair of beat up, high-top construction boots served as the goal. A pair of white low-top sneakers marked the other goal. I had never played with anything but a real hockey net! What could I do, though?

Suddenly the puck was tossed down and J.B. was past me. They didn't even drop the puck for a face-off! J.B. skated straight to the pair of sneakers on the ice and slid the puck through.

"Jason, where were you?" Guy yelled. "You should have been on him!"

"I was waiting for the face-off. I wasn't ready."

"You hire the referees and we'll have face-offs. Until then, be ready!"

Chad was skating with the puck for our team and slid a pass to Gary. Gary back-handed a pass to me. It was a little ahead of me, but I got to it. Two of our opponents charged toward me, Ben and another guy. Quickly I turned directions and began skating backwards toward my own goal.

"Wrong way!" one of my teammates shouted. I thought that it was Chad.

Suddenly, I dug in the inside edge of my left skate and pushed off hard, turning around and flying past the onrushing Ben. The other kid couldn't stop so well, and I flew by him easily. There was just one opponent between me and the goal. I skated straight toward him, and just before getting to him, I faked left and easily pulled the puck around him to the right. I glided in and scored! I raised my stick high above my head.

By the time my stick was down, the five players on the other side were all flying down the ice with my three teammates back alone to stop them. After two quick passes, the puck was sliding between the sneakers.

"Come on, kid!" Guy yelled at me. "You gotta be ready!"

"Sorry. I forgot that there were no face-offs."

The game continued. This time, I was ready. I picked up a loose puck and deked past three guys. *Deke* means to fake a guy out and stick-handle the puck by him. After skating around the third kid, I shot the puck between the skates of the last man. Another goal!

Learning from my earlier mistake, I stayed near the puck, and when the biggest kid on the other team picked it up and began to skate with it, I lifted up his stick and stole the puck from him. I did a sharp hockey turn to my left and sprinted to their goal. The short kid from the other team, J.B., was right behind me. He was their fastest guy, but I knew that I could beat him.

"Jason!" Guy called out from my left, smacking his stick on the ice.

I knew that he wanted a pass but one more goal and I had a hat trick. It would be easy. And then I was on the ice! J.B. had tripped me! A kid on the other team picked up the loose puck and passed it up to J.B. who fired a quick goal.

"I was tripped!" I yelled. "That doesn't count!"

"You should have passed it," Guy said, sounding mad at me.

"But I was tripped! Don't you guys have penalties?"

J.B., the captain of the other team, heard me and said, "Where's the ref, snot-nose?"

How could they play without penalties and without face-offs?

In an instant, Chad was skating for us with the puck when it was stripped away by J.B.. I'd stop him. I skated as fast as I could and overtook J.B. as he sprinted toward our goal. I stepped in front and forced his body to the side just as my coach had taught me.

J.B. slipped and fell hard on the ice. I picked up the loose puck and easily took it up ice and scored. A hat trick!

I was immediately ready to play but none of the other boys were. They were standing around J.B..

J.B. was curled up on the ice, crying, "My knee! My knee!"

"What'd you do that for?" one of the kids on the other team asked me angrily.

"I did nothing wrong!" I snapped back. "No ref in the league would call me on that. Besides, he should have been wearing shin pads, and he'd be fine. I was just playing the body."

"Jason, this is pond hockey. None of us has equipment. You can't play the body," Ben said.

"Well, I was just tripped a minute ago. What about that?"

"You never would have been tripped if you had passed the puck," Guy responded. "I thought that you knew hockey."

"You call this hockey? No refs. No penalties. No uniforms. No scoreboard. No equipment. No goals. No boards. And the ice stinks! You guys don't know what real hockey is."

J.B. was slowly attempting to stand, his face a grimace of pain.

"You all right?" the kids asked.

"Yeah," J.B. said. "Just get this maniac outta here. He doesn't want to play hockey. He's just here to put on a show. Let him go play with the little kids over there. They'll be impressed. It was a lot more fun before he came."

"Yeah," a kid on the other team said.

"Sure," echoed another guy.

"Absolutely," Chad added.

"You heard them," Guy said. "Get lost."

That was it? No more hockey?

"I wouldn't want to play with you guys anyway. You don't know who you just kicked out of your game. None of you guys could even make my team back home. Why would I want to play with you?"

I turned away from the big boys and skated back toward my bag.

Chapter 12

ONE STEP AT A TIME, I told myself. Once again, I wondered if I should just put my hockey bag down on the side of the road and return for it later. Aunt Susan or someone could give me a ride to come back and get it. But what if it got stolen? No, I couldn't chance it. It was too valuable. Besides, I had to be practically home by now. Maybe around the next corner I'd see the house.

The last glimmer of brightness disappeared behind the distant elms and sycamores to the west. The night sky had arrived in full. A shiver crept up my spine. I had never liked the dark very much, and this road was almost pitch black. There were very few streetlights and not many houses. The only steady light was a dim moon sitting low in the sky.

The headlights of an oncoming car or truck approached. I ducked behind a tree. I didn't want a stranger stopping when I was so alone out in the country. When it had gone past, I returned to the side of the road. As the hum of the engine faded in the distance, the eerie stillness of the night started to unnerve me. They don't have quiet like this back around Boston.

I let my bag drop to the ground and tried to drag it. Maybe that would be easier on my arms. But no, it was even harder. I'll go back to the right arm, I said to myself. I grabbed the strap of the hockey bag and slung it over my right shoulder. My eyes focused on the turn in the road up ahead. It looked familiar. This must be the final turn before the Reese house. I was sure of it, but I had thought the same thing about each of the last five turns as well.

I was hot and tired, and every muscle in my body ached. The cool evening breeze did not penetrate my hockey armor. Please let this turn be the last turn, I pleaded. I can't go any further! Step by step, I approached the bend. And then I spotted the bright white light over the front door. The Reese house! The hockey bag didn't seem so heavy over my shoulder anymore as I did a lop-sided jog to the house. I staggered up the front stairs, dropped my bag on the doorstep and practically fell through the door in exhaustion.

Sally stood there staring at me open-mouthed. Jeannie scampered in and stood next to her sister, her eyes glued to me as well.

"Is that Jason?" Aunt Susan's voice boomed from the kitchen.

"Yup!" Sally answered. "And Billy was right. He was playing hockey." There was a trace of a smile at the corner of her mouth.

"Hockey," Jeannie said.

Billy and George flew downstairs, Billy's eyes alive with the eager anticipation of a spectator at a gladiator fight. "You've done it now," Billy whispered to me.

Henry came down the stairs next. He just shook his head.

Aunt Susan stomped red-faced into the front hall and just glared at me. But she said nothing, which made me even more nervous. Seconds seemed to last forever. My words finally broke the silence.

"I'm sorry, Aunt Susan," I said humbly.

"Hockey?" she spit out, her massive body trembling. "I don't know what to say. What you did was so wrong! You had a responsibility! In this family, we take responsibility seriously. We need *everyone*'s help for certain jobs. Your mother counted on us to be here for you. We were. That's what families are for. We count on you as well, and you weren't there."

"I can't pick very much, anyway, Aunt Susan."

"It doesn't matter!" she screeched. "We expect you to do what you can. No more. And you didn't do that!"

I hung my head in shame.

Aunt Susan caught her breath and continued in a calmer tone. "Working the land is what binds us together, Jason. It's our heritage. We used to have our language. And our religion was at the center of our lives. No more. All we have left as Acadians are family and land. That's why the harvest is so important."

The front door opened. It was Big John.

"*D'où sors-tu?* Where have you been?" my uncle exploded.

"Playing hockey," I said, the image of a strap creeping into my brain. "I'm sorry."

"I just drove all the way to the fill and back. It was dark, and there was no one there! How did you get home?"

"Walked."

"All the way from the fill? Why didn't I see you?"

"I guess that I was way over on the side." I was embarrassed to admit that I was afraid of strangers in cars and that I'd hidden from all passing vehicles.

"Go to your room, *vas-y*!" he said in a calm but dead serious tone. "If you were my boy, I'd take some skin off that behind of yours. So just stay up there. There will be no dinner tonight for you. *Monte l'échelle*!"

I wasn't sure what he said, but from the tone of his voice, I guessed it was something like 'Get out of here!' He actually said, "Go upstairs." *Echelle* meant ladder originally but was now used to mean stairs. Acadians have lots of words that originate from their previous life as seafarers. They had ladders, not stairs, on ships. And so when they moved onto the land and into houses they kept their old word. *Au large* is another term like that. In France, it meant the open sea. When the Acadians left the sea and settled in their North American farms, they brought the term *au large* with them, except it referred to their new place of work, the fields.

Anyway, I turned and ran up the stairs and into my room. Why had I skipped potato picking? It now seemed like such a stupid thing to do. I could have played hockey in another day or two. I should have just waited! I was upset about being yelled at, and I felt guilty about letting the family down. I hadn't realized how important the harvest was. I just lay on my bed in all my hockey equipment. I wanted to cry but couldn't. I was angry at myself. I was upset about the hockey. And I was beginning to get very hungry. It had been a terrible day. About the worst in my life. And I wanted my mother.

My father used to yell at me, especially when I was making noise when he was trying to work. He'd get irritated a lot, but I had never seen real anger in his eyes, not as I had just seen in Big John's eyes. I knew that I had done something awful, much worse than simply skipping a chore. The harvest seemed to mean so much to the Reese family.

Was there anything that was as important to my parents? I couldn't think of a thing. Even school wasn't as serious to them. The one time I had skipped a day, they had gotten madder about the wasted tuition than anything else.

My life back home felt suddenly empty. I had my hockey, which I loved, but my parents didn't feel the same way about it. And while I hated picking potatoes, I knew that there was something special about the harvest to the Reeses, and to all the people up here. To all of them except my father.

Then Henry strolled into the bedroom, trying hard to look casual. He walked across the floor and sat down next to me on the bed.

"How was hockey?"

"Terrible."

"Really? I thought that you were good," Henry said.

"I am. Too good, I guess. Kids got mad because I didn't pass the puck. I'm not used to playing without whistles and referees, and so I made some mistakes. Then I ran into this kid, J.B., and he hurt his knee and they blamed me. They don't want me to play with them again."

"That's all right. I don't usually play with them. I play on the other side of the ice with the younger kids and some of the girls. They're a little nicer. The big guys just want me if they don't have enough players. But I really like playing with the younger kids better. You can play with us."

I forced a smile to my face. "Thanks," I said. "Can you go down and get my stuff?"

Henry went downstairs and lugged my hockey bag back up to our room.

"I have to break in these new skates better," I told Henry. "My feet are a little bit sore."

"How do you break them in better?"

"I once heard that Bobby Orr used to sleep wearing his new skates to help break them in. I wonder if that would work?"

"Try and see," Henry suggested.

I slid my hard rubber skate guards over the blades and then put my skates on. Lacing them tightly was a lot of work, but I did it. Pretty tightly, anyway.

The rest of the evening, I just lay around on my bed, skates on, and relived that terrible day. Hunger pangs worked their way from my stomach to my brain but were usually pushed aside by that sick feeling of having messed up so badly.

I suppose that it can't get any worse, I thought, as I finally dozed off to sleep.

Chapter 13

THE HOT, DELICIOUS MOZZARELLA cheese dripping from the pepperoni pizza just begged to be attacked. The irresistible aroma filled the room and drove me toward the food. I craned my neck to look up. The pizza rested high on top of a shiny white counter. I grasped for it but couldn't quite touch it. I was so hungry! Nothing had ever smelled so good! I stood on my tiptoes and reached up as high as I could, stretching every muscle in my body. Just when I was sure I would grab a slice, the counter top seemed further away, the pizza more out of reach. Was it a mirage?

Suddenly someone whacked my hand.

"Stop it," a voice yelled.

I opened my eyes. It was George, in the bunk above me, pushing my hand away.

"What are you doing, you pervert!" George barked at me.

I looked around. Where was the pizza? Why was I reaching up to the top of George's bunk? And then it hit me. It was just a dream! I had a foggy recollection of dreaming about food all night, and I realized how starved I was. I was so hungry that I felt I could eat anything! Even spaghetti and clam sauce, the worst thing my mother ever made me eat. I had once read a story about a kid trying to survive alone in the woods. He ate live bugs and raw rabbits. I used to wonder how anyone could do something like that. I always said that I'd starve before eating bugs and raw meat. Well, at last I understood how someone could do it.

"What's wrong with you?" George asked.

"Sorry. It was just a dream. I thought that you were a pizza."

Henry laughed from across the room. "Pizza face," he whispered.

"What did you say?" George snapped.

"Nothing."

"Huh?" George asked.

"I'm so hungry," I complained.

"Then go down to the kitchen and snag a bite," George said in a friendly voice.

"And get in trouble, right," I said.

"No, really. My mom is up. She gets up at 5:00 every morning. She'll give you something."

I looked at the clock. It said 5:45. As I swung my feet off the bed and onto the floor, I realized that I had worn my hockey skates all night. The hard rubber skate guards landed on the pine floor boards and I stood up. I took two steps forward, then found myself flat on my face. Ow!

George was doubled over in laughter. I looked to Henry. Even Henry was smiling, trying hard to hide his laughter. I turned my head and saw that one of my skate laces was attached to the post of my bed.

"What did you do that for?" I hissed at George.

It was another minute before George could stop laughing. "You were confined to your room. Just wanted to make sure that you didn't get into any more trouble. You know, with your sleepwalking and all."

I had landed right on my left knee, and it ached.

"I don't sleepwalk," I lied. My mother had warned my aunt that I sometimes did sleepwalk at night. It was usually when I had to go the bathroom really bad. I had watered a few closets in mistaken attempts to find the bathroom. But I didn't want my cousins to know about that.

There was a rapid pounding up the stairs and then a knock on the door. No one said anything. Aunt Susan knocked again and then entered. "Jason, what are you doing?" she asked looking down at me on the floor.

"He's going for a morning skate, Mom," George chuckled.

I detected traces of a grin at the corners of my aunt's mouth. "Jason Quinn, your mother said that you were a hockey fanatic, but isn't this too much?" she said with mock seriousness. "Skates weren't meant for pine board floors and certainly not for old ones with big cracks like this one has. Get those skates off before you kill yourself and get downstairs for breakfast."

"But Aunt Susan, it wasn't the pine boards that did it."

"Huh?" she asked.

I glanced up at George still sitting high on top of the upper bunk. All signs of humor were gone from his face.

"Nothing," I said. Couldn't she see my skate lace tied to the bed?

"Just come on down. You must be ravenous. And it's a school morning, remember? And make sure you do your chore today."

Aunt Susan left the room. I almost expected that George would thank me for not saying anything, but George didn't say a word. I just took my skates off and went downstairs to the kitchen.

Breakfast was hot oatmeal with brown sugar and milk on top. I had always avoided oatmeal before. It was too gray and gross-looking. But at this moment, I would have eaten anything, and so I didn't complain when Aunt Susan placed a full, steaming bowl of it in front of me. I took a little bite and burned my tongue! I dropped my spoon onto the table, splattering the uneaten oatmeal still on the spoon.

"Sorry," I said sheepishly.

"Take small spoonfuls from the side, and blow on it," Aunt Susan said calmly as she handed me a damp sponge. I cleaned up the bits of oatmeal from around my place, and then I cautiously scooped the hot cereal as my aunt had suggested.

Wow, was it good! I ate two heaping bowlfuls, attacking it by the end of my second serving. One by one, the chairs around me filled, and the kitchen came alive with chatter, laughter, and normal table bickering. I barely heard it. Food was all I could think about. I didn't stop eating until my stomach felt like a basketball.

I was glad that oatmeal was one food that there was always plenty of. I still cringed whenever I thought about my second dinner with the Reeses. Dinner that night had been *pot-en-pot*, which is an Acadian meat stew, plus we had extra potatoes on the side. I had asked for seconds of the meat stew when there was none. Aunt Susan had politely directed me to have seconds of potatoes, but I had insisted that I wanted more meat. Someone finally had to say that there was usually enough meat for only one helping, but there was always plenty of potato or pasta to fill up on.

After eating breakfast, I tried to do an especially good job sweeping the back hall. And then as I went out the door on my way to school, I turned to my aunt and said, "I really am sorry about yesterday. I wanted to play hockey so badly, and I know that it was wrong. I won't do it again. I'll be there to pick today and whenever you need me."

"Thank you for saying that, Jason," Aunt Susan said kindly, holding my face in her small, chubby hands. "I do believe you mean that. The harvest might be done by this afternoon. We might not need you. And I meant to ask you, how was your first day of school?"

"Pretty good, except for French. We only learned Spanish at Charter Hall, and so I didn't know a word of the French."

"French in school," Aunt Susan muttered, almost to herself. "When I was a kid, you weren't allowed to speak French in school. My parents spoke mostly French at home, and so I let it slip sometimes at school. One teacher got so fed up with me that she finally made me write 'I will not speak French at school' 150 times. Ay-yuh."

The thought of my Aunt Susan being punished made me laugh.

"Now the schools up here are pushing the French. They don't want us to lose our culture. Plus, they say knowing two languages can help a kid get into college or get a scholarship. Thirty years ago they said it was important to be like everyone else. Now we're supposed to be different. I don't know."

I smiled at my aunt. I wasn't sure if I should ask the question that popped into my head. But the words just came out.

"Hey, Aunt Susan, did my dad change his name because he was ashamed of being French?"

A sad look came over her face.

"I'm not quite sure," she said. "Your father did want to be just plain old American. So he changed the 'e' in Quine to an 'n.' I don't think that he was ashamed. But he was afraid that people in his new life would look at him differently with such a French-sounding name. It was a small change, Jason, and the name sounds the same either way. Anyway, listen to me rambling on! You have to get going. I do need to say something, though. I think that you should take a week before playing hockey again. I think that's a fair punishment."

I nodded in agreement. It was fair. And also, since I couldn't play with the older boys, it really didn't matter. It didn't matter if I would ever play again.

Chapter 14

"GOAL!" I SCREAMED, HIGH-FIVING Jeannie. "That was an awesome goal, Jeannie."

"Goal!" my three year-old cousin echoed, beaming.

"Just drop the puck," George growled.

"And I think that you should let Jeannie control three of the guys, not just two," Billy said.

"You two guys are much older than Jeannie and me! We can do whatever we want!"

"You've played this game more than everyone in this family put together," George argued.

"Jeannie, do you have your right hand on the goalie?" I asked.

Jeannie grabbed the rubber knob at the far right of the table hockey game and nodded. Her other hand controlled the right wing.

I looked at the electronic scoreboard above the dome. HOME 9 to VISITORS 5. I had argued that it wasn't fair that I got stuck with little Jeannie on my team, but George and Billy had insisted. And so I badly wanted to win. Controlling the two defensemen and two of the forwards, I had pretty much protected the goal on my own. Still, Jeannie had come up with a few really good saves. Probably luck, but that was okay. George and Billy had begun getting mad and arguing with each other. I was really enjoying this.

"What a game, Jeannie! One more goal and we win the seventh and deciding game of the Stanley Cup finals! Set?" I asked my older cousins.

"Set?" Jeannie asked.

George and Billy nodded intently.

"When can I play?" Sally whined, hanging over the game as she watched.

"After!" I snapped. "Just get out of the way so we can see." She was always bugging me to play with her.

I pressed the center face-off button and the puck automatically rolled up the side chute and dropped at center ice. Quick as lightning, I flicked the knob of my center forward and sent the small plastic puck flying toward the opposing goal. It ricocheted off the goalie. They hadn't even moved it! Pure luck.

"Move your guy," I yelled to Jeannie. "Push it in all the way!"

Jeannie did that, but George's defenseman had already dug the puck out of the corner and was firing it blindly up ice. He doesn't even pass it to one of his guys, I thought. He just blasts it in my direction.

A ring sounded from the other room. Another ring. Seconds later, Aunt Susan walked into the den.

"Jason, telephone. It's your mother."

"Time out," I said. I trotted into the other room and got on the phone.

"Hello?"

"Jason?"

"Oh, hi, Mom. When are you going to come back?" I asked over the phone.

"I'm not sure. Things are pretty complicated down here."

"Is there money for my hockey tour?"

"Not yet. I'm sorry. Jason, I wish that you wouldn't ask that first thing every time we talk. I do have more important things to worry about. I hope that it happens, but please do not count on it."

I felt pangs of disappointment. After a brief pause, I said, "What about money for youth hockey up here?"

"The nearest rink is fifty miles away. I've told you, that's too far. I can't ask your Aunt Susan or Uncle John to cart you there four times a week. That's four hundred miles of driving! And the money for the program is even more than the cost at home. Things might be different next year. Let's hope so."

I felt sick. No real hockey all winter!

"What about outdoor hockey?" my mother asked me. "I thought that Susan said they play a lot of pond hockey up there."

"I played once, a few weeks ago. It wasn't very good. And then it got warm and the ice melted."

"Just be careful, Jason. I knew a boy who fell through the ice and drowned when I was a kid. Anyway, it's supposed to be very cold this week. They're saying that we might get record lows before Thanksgiving down here in Boston."

"Really?"

"How's school, Jason?"

"It's okay. I'm getting used to having kids from different grades with me. And my teacher is pretty nice, even if she is strict. It's a lot different from Charter Hall. But most of the kids are okay."

"You getting along all right with your cousins?"

I didn't know what to say. Sure, it was better than the first day. They could be a little rough, and they still played lots of jokes on me. Henry was nice. But even George and Billy sometimes played with me and I'd have fun. And George did get in a fight with that older kid in school who had made fun of my dad. When I had thanked him, George just shrugged me off and said that it was nothing personal. Family honor forced him to do it. Still, it made me feel good.

"Yeah, I guess," I said, answering her question. I was getting along better with them.

"Good," my mother said. She probably had guessed that it wasn't great but didn't want to know more. "I hope that you're not giving your aunt or uncle any trouble."

"Naw. I do what Aunt Susan says. Big John is away for a few weeks working at a logging camp somewhere south. When are you going to be back here?"

"I'm not sure. Soon, I hope."

"Mom, you first said it would be just a couple of weeks. Then you said it would be another week or so. Now you don't know!"

There was a pause on the other end of the line.

"Jason, I'll do my best. Trust me, please."

"Just try to come up here soon. And please try to get me on that Canadian Hockey Tour for my February vacation. Please."

"I'll try, Jason. Bye."

"Bye, Mom."

I hung up and ran into the kitchen.

"Aunt Susan, is it true that the weather's going to get real cold?"

"That's what they say," my aunt said without breaking her rhythm scrubbing the kitchen counter.

There had been just three days of skating all fall so far, and I had been grounded and missed two of them. In the last month, the temperature hadn't stayed below freezing for long enough.

"Goal!" Billy screamed from the den.

I scrambled into the other room and saw George and Billy high-fiving each other. I looked at the scoreboard of the hockey game. HOME 9 - VISITOR 10.

"That's not fair! I said 'time out!'"

"You got your two minute time out," Billy explained calmly. "Then you weren't ready, so we just continued. Jeannie played a great game, but she just wasn't up to the task. Good effort, though."

I looked angrily at Jeannie. "How could you let them play without me!" I snapped at my little cousin.

Jeannie's smile turned into a frown and she looked up at me with her big brown eyes and said, "Sorry."

I was so mad! "Let's play again," I finally said.

"How can we play again? You said that this was the seventh and deciding game. We won. Better luck next year."

George and Billy got up and walked out of the room, fists raised in the air.

"Can I play now?" Sally asked.

It wouldn't be fun playing with just Sally and Jeannie. Even though Sally was seven, she wasn't very good at this game.

"Where's Henry?"

"Here I am," Henry said, walking into the room. "Heard you got whooped."

"Those guys cheated. They kept on playing when I was on the phone with my mother. It's not fair."

Henry just shrugged his shoulders. "How about me and Sally against you and Jeannie, and Jeannie has to control three guys," he asked.

"All right," I agreed, resetting the scores to zeros. Sally beamed.

"Aw right," Jeannie said.

I pressed the center face-off button, the puck dropped and the two plastic centers spun wildly.

Chapter 15

"THEY SHOULD MAKE AN announcement any minute," Henry said to me as he stuffed the last piece of peanut butter sandwich into his mouth.

"How does he know whether it's safe?" I asked.

Henry garbled something with his mouth full and made a cranking motion with his fist as if he were using an egg beater.

"Huh?"

He chewed a little more, then swallowed. "Mr. Bailey drills a hole into the ice. If it's eight inches thick, then it's okay. Otherwise we have to wait."

I tried to imagine the principal of my old school, Mrs. Addams, drilling a hole through ice to see if it was safe for skating. Mrs. Addams was not the sports type. I couldn't even picture it.

As if on cue, into the classroom marched the principal. Mr. Bailey was a tall muscular man. Mostly bald, he had more hair on his face than on his head. A bushy brown mustache hung over his upper lip. Mr. Bailey was usually smiling or joking with kids. You could often hear his deep laugh echo through the school corridors.

"Excuse me, children," the principal said. He spoke softly but with authority, and the class quieted down almost immediately. "I have just returned from the pond, and I wanted to let you know that the depth of the ice is currently ..."

Mr. Bailey paused and looked into the eyes of the eager children in the classroom. He smiled, clearly enjoying the drama he was building.

"... nine inches!"

"Yaaay!" the boys and girls cheered.

Skating, today, at the big pond! It didn't matter that I wouldn't be able to play hockey with the older guys. It had been so long since I had skated, I just wanted to get out on the ice.

The rest of the day dragged. Geography, math, art. I couldn't focus on anything but skating. Getting on the bus at the end of the day, Guy and J.B. spoke loudly about the great game of hockey that they were going to have. Then they looked at me, and both of them seemed to smirk. Even that couldn't dampen my spirits. I loved to skate and that was enough. For the moment, anyway.

On the bus ride home, Henry told me his mom usually drove all the kids to the pond when there was skating, and they stayed until it got dark. The bus pulled to a stop at 3:00.

"We should be at the ice by three-thirty," Henry said.

"So that should give us about an hour and a half to play," I said.

I was the first out of the bus, and in seconds I was in my room, rummaging through my hockey equipment. What should I bring? Not all of my equipment this time. I decided to put on my shin pads underneath sweat pants. And I'd wear my cup. That was my most important piece of protection, and no one would see it. Plus I'd bring my gloves and stick. I felt nervous about skating without a helmet, but none of the other kids had helmets, so I wouldn't bring mine. I was ready!

I ran out of the bedroom and started downstairs while Billy, George, Alice and Henry dug out their skates from various closets. Only Jeannie and Sally would stay behind with their mother.

"Mom, can I go too?" Sally asked Aunt Susan, who was leaning against the banister at the foot of the stairs.

"I don't know," my aunt said with a hint of hesitation. "I can't be there today to look after you. Why don't you just stay home.

You can watch whatever you want on TV. You won't have to fight with your brothers about it."

"I don't want to watch TV! Please let me go! I'm a good skater. I went all the time last year!"

"But not alone with the kids," Aunt Susan said.

"Alice will be there, and I'm almost as old as Jason and Henry. Henry was seven and went alone two years ago." Sally stared stubbornly at her mother.

"Henry's a boy."

"Who cares?"

Aunt Susan hesitated, and Sally smiled. She knew she had won.

"Okay," my aunt sighed. "Just be careful and stay with your sister the whole time. Now go get your stuff!"

Sally raced up the stairs.

"Let's go!" Aunt Susan called from the back door. "It'll be dark before you know it!"

I sprinted upstairs. "Hurry guys!" I called from the top step, then ran down just as quickly. Aunt Susan placed a hand on my shoulder and smiled at me. Seconds later, my five cousins barreled down the stairs, fighting to be first.

"Whoa," Aunt Susan cried. "Just slow down and get into the car."

We all piled into their old brown station wagon, and then we were off. Spy Pond in Glenville was about two miles away. I had been by there twice before, but not when there was ice. As the car slowed down, my heart beat faster. Out the window my eyes were drawn to a smooth sheet of ice that seemed to stretch out forever. It sparkled like glass reflecting the sun's low rays. Surrounded by majestic pine trees and full hemlocks under a deep blue sky, I was sure that I had never seen anything so beautiful. And we were the first ones there!

Aunt Susan stopped the car. The gang practically rolled out and raced down to a splintery old bench next to the pond. I put on my skates as fast as I could. Aunt Susan was helping Henry and Sally tie their skates while the older boys tied their own. I hardly paid any attention. I wanted to be the first one on the ice. I tugged hard at the laces of my left skate, then tied a knot. I did the same with my right skate. Other cars pulled up as I put on my hockey gloves, grabbed my puck, and dropped down to my knees to crawl the five feet over frozen dirt to the ice.

I stood up on my skates and pushed off. The ice was beautiful! It was smoother than any rink ice I had ever been on. I skated toward the middle of the pond. And skated. And skated. The ice never stopped! It was unbelievable. I kept skating and skating as fast as I could, then dropped my puck and began to stick-handle. And I kept on going straight. After what seemed like forever, I approached the other side of the pond and turned around. The kids back at the bench looked like tiny specks. I couldn't believe how big the ice was!

I began to skate back to the rest of the kids. When I got near the bench, all of my cousins were skating, and about six other kids were there too. Guy and J.B. and the other older boys were all getting their skates on. I wished that I could play with them, but just being there was awesome.

"Jason, pass me the puck!" Alice called out.

I slid the puck very slowly to my thirteen year-old cousin, expecting her to miss it. But she caught it on her stick and fired it right back to me. Wow! She's pretty good, I thought.

"She's better than me," Henry said as if he could read my thoughts.

I passed the puck to Henry this time, and he fumbled it, getting it caught in his skates. When he finally dug it out, he batted it to Alice who handled it smoothly and fired it back to me.

I kept reminding myself that I couldn't be a show-off with these kids. The older boys didn't want to play with me anymore. I didn't want the younger kids to hate me too. Henry, Alice and I continued our three-way game of catch until Sally skated over to join us.

"Can I play, too?"

"Sure," Alice said, sliding her younger sister a pass. Like Henry, Sally missed it, losing the puck in her skates, awkwardly twisting her stick to get at it.

"Use your skates to help you, Sally," I said, "Block the puck with the flat side of your blade and kick it out to your stick. Pass it to me, and I'll show you how."

Sally finally got the puck and slid it over to me. I skated forward a step so that the puck would go right into my skates. I turned my left skate, and the puck stopped dead. I kicked the puck forward a little, right onto my stick, and I flicked a crisp pass to Alice. Alice passed it back to me.

"Try and do it like that, Sally. Here."

I passed the puck slowly to Sally. She turned her skate exactly as I had demonstrated, and she stopped it perfectly.

"Awesome!" she squealed.

I beamed back at her. "Great job, Sally."

Sally passed the puck to Henry who tried to skate around it to receive it on the left side of his stick. He missed it.

"Use your backhand, Henry," I instructed my cousin. "That's the other side of your stick. Alice, get the puck and pass to Henry's backhand."

Alice sprinted after the loose puck, returned with it, and slid a soft pass to Henry. He kept his stick flat on the ice and stopped it with his backhand.

"That's right," I said, encouraged by my cousins' learning and my teaching. I was feeling a little like a coach and it felt good.

After about fifteen minutes of passing the puck with Alice, Sally and Henry, I noticed that the older boys had begun their game a little further down on the ice. Billy and George were playing with them. They weren't too bad. If they had real skates, they'd probably be decent. But no one could skate well on the junk they had on their feet. By this time, there were about eight other kids standing around, watching me help my cousins. Five of them were girls ranging in age from seven to twelve. Three of them were in my class at school. The others were boys a little younger than me.

"Can we play too?" one of the boys asked.

"Sure," I said.

"Can we have a game?" one of the other boys asked.

"In a while. Let's do some practicing first."

No one objected.

"Put down your pucks first," I instructed. "And follow me. I want you all to work on long strides. Push off with your left skate. Dig deeply into the ice, push as hard as you can, and glide. Then do the same thing with your right skate. Just follow me."

I led the way with the others trying to follow my lead. After ten minutes of that drill, I stopped.

"Great job, you guys!" They really had improved quickly. "Now let's work on your stopping. Sprint for twenty steps, and then stop as hard as you can on your left edges."

I watched as all the kids tried to do what I said. Only Alice actually stopped cleanly on both left edges. Three kids slowed down a little using their left edges. Two used a right edge to stop. The rest just didn't stop.

"If you can't stop, try this," I said patiently. I then skated forward and turned my skates inward, leaning into both inner edges. It was a snowplow stop, the stop people first learn on skis.

The kids who couldn't stop tried again, with two actually slowing to a stop using the snowplow.

"Great!" I said.

I led the group through figure-eights, checking out the crossover skills of my skaters. Some did okay, but with decent ankle support from their skates they could do ten times better.

After twenty more minutes of drills, I called the skaters in.

"Time for a game now."

"Yeah!" the kids cheered.

I put myself on the team with most of the beginning skaters and began the game by tossing the puck to Alice on the opposing team. Alice skated hard toward me. I could have stick-checked her and taken the puck away, but it didn't seem like the right thing to do. Instead, I just backed up toward my own goal. She fired and I stopped it with my skate.

"Here, Sally!" I said, sliding the puck forward to her.

The pass was short, but Sally used her skate to stop it and she kicked it forward to herself.

"Yeah, Sally!" I said, following her up ice. These kids weren't like the guys back home, but I was having fun!

Chapter 16

"JASON, ARE YOU GOING to be at the pond today?" little Helena asked as I headed for the school bus.

"Of course," I said and grinned. It was only about the tenth time that someone had asked me that today.

"Yay! Your cousin's awesome," Helena said to Sally who was skipping right behind me on her way to the bus.

Sally beamed proudly. For a month, there had been excellent ice each day. Billy and George couldn't remember this many great skating days in a row. The pond was so huge that when one part got too scraped up, we just moved our skating to a new section. And between the wind at night and the slight melting in the afternoon sun, even the used sections seemed to smooth themselves out without a Zamboni! I couldn't believe how much fun pond skating was.

Each afternoon was about the same. Bus ride home. Get dressed. Pile into the car. Head to the pond. And skate. The few times that Aunt Susan was busy and couldn't drive us, we just walked. It was a forty-five minute walk with the little kids, but usually someone who knew my cousins stopped to give us a ride. Everybody pretty much knew everybody else in Glenville, and carrying sticks and skates, it was obvious where we were headed.

The sun shone. It was cold but not frigid, another beautiful afternoon for hockey. Each day the same group of kids showed up for "practice" with me. They all worked hard to learn what I demonstrated for them. Alice had gotten so much better in just a month. She had been the best the first day, but with some tips from me and almost two hours of skating each day for four weeks, she was becoming an amazing hockey player. She could do some things even better than me! I shouldn't have been surprised, after seeing how quickly she moved her hands when she picked potatoes. Alice loved hockey and was proud to be the only girl in the group who wore hockey skates. The rest of the girls had figure skates.

Some of the other kids were pretty good, too. Henry was probably the next best. He was a good stick-handler and could skate pretty fast, but his skates were so lousy that he had no ankle support for crossovers or good stops. I wished that I could get Henry a decent pair of skates. Sally was probably a better skater than Henry even though she was two years younger, but she wasn't as good at stick-handing, passing and shooting. She only wore figure skates and had never played hockey until this winter.

Sally's friends, Helena and Gina, weren't very good. They couldn't stop at all. But they loved to skate and play hockey, or try to play anyway.

Alice's friend Maddy was a year younger than Alice, only twelve. Her full name was Madeline but nobody ever called her that. Maddy had never skated much before, but she had improved more than anyone. I had seen her play basketball in the school yard with the guys. She was better than most of the boys her age. She must be a natural athlete, I decided, and she was addicted to hockey. Her game sense and quickness with her stick were impressive. She had even learned to deke!

The other boys in the group were Danny, Ricky and Ross. Danny was ten, like me. He was nervous and afraid to try new things but still loved playing. Ricky was seven and a pretty good player, but he had to wear figure skates, hand-me-downs from his older sister. Ross DuBois was only six, but he was amazing. He was the only one with a decent pair of skates, and he could fly, weaving in and out of kids twice his size. Ross was born to skate. His little legs moved twice as fast as anyone else's. He wasn't strong with his stick, but he was only six. He'd be awesome some day. He reminded me a little of myself when I was that age. Little Ross was fearless too. His gutsiness and grace always made me smile. Ross was Guy's little brother. Guy also had good skates. And he was the best of the older boys, but Ross would be even better some day. I savored that thought.

The older boys just played their game each day, ignoring us.

"What are we doing today?" Ross asked eagerly after his brother Guy finished tying his skates.

"Stick-handing and skating, and looking up at the same time if you can," I answered. I had worked out a whole sequence of drills in my head. And, as always, we would end with a game.

"Over here, with your pucks," I called out to my gang, leading the way to a fresh section of ice. I demonstrated how to stick-handle and look up at the same time. They all watched intently. They seemed to really enjoy being coached by me!

"In a game, if you stick-handle with your head down, you can't see where the defense is and where your teammates are. I've seen more 2-on-0's or 2-on-1's which have failed because the pass wasn't made. And if you're not looking up, you can't see what to do and you won't make the pass."

The kids all nodded enthusiastically. Suddenly the image of me not passing to Daryl popped into my head, and I felt embarrassed. I knew that I should have passed that puck.

"I want you all to try it with a puck, going down to the cabin and back. Try to stick-handle and not look down. It's hard, so don't worry if you can't do it right away. And one at a time, take a break on the side with me, and I'll sharpen your skates with my stone."

I had brought my sharpening stone to the pond today. I had gotten it in my stocking last Christmas, and I kept it in my bag for temporary edges before a game if I didn't get a chance to really sharpen my skates. Now it was all I had. The nearest skate sharpening place was a sporting goods store in Mill Creek, the town next to Glenville, ten miles away. Mill Creek was the town which played Glenville each year in a game of pickup hockey with kids in the eighth grade and younger. Mill Creek had beaten Glenville for the last five years, and Guy and Billy were determined to stop that streak this year. The game was played each February vacation if there was ice. The kids called it the Lower Valley Championship because Glenville and Mill Creek were the only towns in the Lower Valley.

One by one, the children in my group skated to the side of the pond. I dried their blades and ran my stone up and down the inner and outer edges about a dozen times each. I wished that I could get their skates really sharpened. Even more, I wished that I could get them good skates. But the stone was better than nothing.

Up, down, Up, down. I filed while watching my skaters do as I had instructed. Most kids struggled, but a few did okay. Alice was excellent at it. Maddy and Henry did a good job with this drill as well.

After all the skates were sharpened, I demonstrated 2-on-1 skills, passing back and forth, encouraging the kids to use their backhands as well as their forehands. Then, more stops and starts and crossovers. And finally, the game.

"Today, it's me, Ross, Sally, Gina and Maddy against Alice, Henry, Helena, Danny and Ricky. Set up your goals."

Alice and Maddy, the oldest kids on each team, went to get their boots and set them up for goals.

"You guys take it out," I said, tossing a puck to Henry.

Henry began to stick-handle the puck with Ross trying to skate backwards on defense against him. Alice was to Henry's left, and just as Henry got to Ross, he slipped a pass to his left, right onto Alice's stick. Ross turned and tried to catch up to

Alice, but she hadn't missed a stride. She skated in toward the goal that I was defending. She moved the puck to her left and I moved with her. I can stop a deke left, I thought. And just when I was sure that Alice would shoot, she glided the puck to her right, across the crease. Henry had skated by Ross after passing and was there in front and easily slid the puck between the boots.

I was mad that I hadn't seen that pass coming, but they had done that play exactly as I had showed them. It was beautiful, and I was proud of them.

"Great goal!" I said.

Alice and Henry high-fived each other and skated back to their ends of the ice.

"One to nothing," Danny said.

"We're not keeping score, remember?" I said. Two days before, there had been an argument about whether a puck went over or to the left of a boot. Alice had suggested that we stop keeping score, and then there'd be fewer fights. I hadn't like that idea at first. I thought that it wouldn't be as much fun without keeping score, but I didn't know how else to stop the arguing. So I tried it. And Alice had been right. Once we stopped keeping score, there were no more fights. And surprisingly, the game was just as much fun.

Ross began to stick-handle the puck up ice. As he approached Danny, he tried to shovel a pass to Maddy on his left. He passed a little too slowly and a little too late, and Danny knocked the puck away.

"Nice try," I said from the goal. It was a nice try. 'Good idea, bad execution,' my coach used to say.

Maddy picked up the loose puck and skated with it. It was going to be a great afternoon. We had a good forty-five minutes to play before it got dark. And no subs! On my old team we had three lines and we sat for more time than we played. Not here, though. That was one advantage of pond hockey over youth hockey!

Chapter 17

"MOM!" I SQUEALED AND raced toward the front door.

My mother opened her arms and let me run into them. "It's good to see you again, Jason. I'm sorry that I was away for so long."

She let me go and stepped back to look at me.

"Is it my imagination, or have you grown?"

I smiled. Adults always say stuff like that. But not usually your mother.

"You're looking really great. I mean it. It must be the fresh Maine air," she said.

"So," I asked, "what about the Canadian Hockey Tour? Will I be able to do it?" I peered eagerly into my mother's face.

Mom's eyes narrowed with sympathy and she took a deep breath. Her smile evaporated.

"Oh, Jason," she began.

I knew what the answer would be.

"That tour costs almost one thousand dollars. I just don't have the money right now. Maybe next year."

"Next year I won't be a Squirt. I'll be a Pee Wee, and I won't be one of the oldest kids anymore. This is going to be my year!"

George and Henry stood quietly in the back of the room, trying hard not to look nosy, but I knew that they were taking in every word. I was set to try the Santa Claus argument but thought better of it when I spotted my cousins listening. And I knew that if my mother couldn't afford that tour, Santa wasn't going to come through either.

"Come on up and finish the game, you guys," Billy yelled from the top of the stairs.

Aunt Susan squeezed by Henry who stood in the doorway to the kitchen.

"Ellen, welcome back!" she said warmly and in the same breath hollered upstairs, "His mother's here! And don't yell! Come on down if you have something to say!"

Aunt Susan stepped up to my mother and gave her a polite hug. My mom tried to hug her back but could only wrap her arms about halfway around Aunt Susan's enormous upper body.

"It is good to see you, Susan," Mom said. "I hope that Jason hasn't been too much trouble."

"Trouble?" She gave me a serious, raised eyebrow look, and then broke into a huge smile. "Not at all! He's been great. He's becoming quite the hockey coach, I hear, ay-yuh. He's been terrific working every day with the younger boys and some of the girls."

"Oh, that's great," my mother said, radiating pleasure and pride. "Susan, I can't thank you enough for all you've done."

"He's my brother's boy. He's family. And he's a good boy," my aunt said as she gently mussed my hair.

Billy scampered down the stairs. "You coming, Jay?"

"How about a 'hello' for your Aunt Ellen?" Susan barked, shaking her head in disgust.

"Hello, Aunt Ellen," Billy said automatically.

"Hello, uh, Billy, right?"

Billy nodded.

"Gotta go upstairs, Mom. We need to finish up a game." I ran up after Billy, and George and Henry followed.

"10-9, two minutes to go," Billy declared, slamming the bedroom door and reattaching the mini-basket to the top of the door. The mini-basket was really mini: about the size of my hand. It was free if you sent a UPC seal from a box of cereal. But you did have to pay one dollar for shipping and handling. The basket had looked cool on the back of the package. There was a picture of an NBA star slam-dunking it. Henry and I had each chipped in fifty cents from our potato money to send away for the mini-basketball kit. Billy had told us from the start that it was a rip-off, and so when I first saw the tiny box it came in, I was sure that Billy was right. It was small and plastic and flimsy, but it had actually lasted almost a whole game so far.

Billy had laughed and said it was cheap when we opened it earlier today. But it was Saturday night and snowing hard, and there was nothing else to do, so Billy didn't mind playing with it. It was Billy and Henry against George and me. We had set a wind-up egg timer for fifteen minutes. George and I were down 10-9.

"Hey, wait," George argued. "You can't count that time we went down to see Jason's mother. Set the clock back at least three minutes!"

"No way," Billy insisted. "Time's ticking. You'd better play."

George held the tiny plastic ball between the thumb and index finger of his right hand and looked toward the hoop. Billy covered him, placing a hand on George's shoulder.

"Gimme some room!" George yelled.

Billy ignored him.

George faked to the basket and flicked me a pass. I moved to the hoop and tossed what looked to be a perfect shot. In and out, no basket! I dove for the rebound and Billy leaped on top of me, grabbing at my hands for the tiny ball. Ow! He was heavy. But I was not going to let him get that ball. Henry and George just stood, watching us wrestle. George finally dove in and grabbed Billy and yanked him away. I got up, stepped toward the door and was ready to drop an easy lay-up to tie the score.

Then, wham! This time it was Henry who had jumped on my back and grabbed my arms.

"Shooting foul!" George protested.

Ding! The egg timer went off.

"Game's over," Billy said. "Nice try, fellahs."

"Hey, he was tackled in the middle of a shot!" George cried. "He gets a foul shot! Don't be a jerk, Billy. He got clobbered by Henry. Just ask him."

"Did you foul him?" Billy asked Henry.

Henry nodded yes.

"Okay. One shot. You need to sink it to tie," Billy said, smiling confidently. "From the bunk bed."

"From the rug!" George argued.

"Okay, from the rug," Billy agreed.

"Jason Quinn," Billy announced into his fist, pretending it was a microphone, "at the line, trying to tie it all up. The buzzer has gone off, but the referee has determined that the shooting foul occurred before time expired. This is it, ladies and gentleman. There's no tomorrow and no second chances. We'll see what the Quinn boy is made of."

I stood at the edge of the rug and looked up at the mini-basket. I held the ball softly between my thumb and first two fingers. I really wanted to sink this and beat Billy. I concentrated as hard as I could and gently floated the tiny orange ball up toward the hoop. I felt good about the shot. It bounced off the wooden molding above the door and dropped right down at the basket. It looked like a perfect shot, but seemed to hit the rim and fall wide.

"No good! The game is over!" Billy announced, slapping Henry a high five. "The Quinn kid could not do it. The crowd goes wild!"

How could I miss? I just stood there staring at the mini-basket while Billy opened the door and left, his brothers following him.

I gazed out the window. The snow seemed to light up the night sky but it was falling so heavily that I could still barely see the tree outside my window. I wondered how the snow would affect the hockey. The guys had said that they usually had to shovel if they wanted to play on the pond. If the ice was really hard, someone's dad might bring a plow down to clear off the snow. But they wouldn't clear the whole pond. There'd be no more skating and skating and skating without turning. It would be more like a rink, I thought.

I shut the door and turned to the hoop. Alone in the room, I shot a short, two foot shot. In and out again. How come I couldn't sink a thing? I was upset about the tour. I was mad because of the loss. And I wished that it wasn't snowing. I stepped right up to the door and shot from about one foot away. Another seemingly perfect shot but in and out again.

Hmm. Strange, I thought. I walked across the bedroom and dragged the desk chair up to the doorway. I stood up on the chair and held the plastic ball an inch above the basket and released it. It seemed to bounce on the air above the rim. It then fell wide. Startled, I jumped back a half a step, almost falling off the chair. Was this some weird force like ESP? Actually, telekinesis is the word. It's when you can move something with your mind. I had seen a TV show about it once. I felt a little bit scared but tried it again. I held the ball about an inch above the rim and dropped it. The same thing happened! The ball changed directions in midair! I pulled the mini-basket off the door and examined it closely. There, stretched right across the top of the plastic rim, was a thin piece of transparent scotch tape! So that's what Billy had been doing alone when the rest of us were all downstairs with my mom. For some reason I wasn't angry at my oldest cousin. Instead I was pretty impressed with Billy's scheme. Rather than complain, I would keep quiet. I'd think of a way to even the score. This would be fun.

I left my bedroom and headed down the stairs to look for my mom. As I turned to go into the kitchen, I heard her speaking in a hushed voice to my aunt. I stopped and listened.

"I don't know what we'll do!" my mother whispered. "He's used to having everything. I'm used to having everything! It'll be a hard adjustment."

"No it won't, Ellen," Aunt Susan said quietly. "He's doing great here, and we're not exactly rolling in money."

"I suppose. He did look good. But Albert always thought that it was so important that we provide him with every advantage."

"Ellen, honey, that was Albert's problem! He was always bothered about us being poor. He was the only one of the eight of us like that. I can't explain it. We had everything we needed growing up. Sure, we all worked hard on the farm. Stopped school completely for the harvest back then, even first grade. We did it all by hand. But we always had food on the table. What more did we need? But it was never enough for Albert. I always wondered where his Acadian blood was. He hated physical work. Did anything to get out of potato picking. Maybe that was it. But boy was he smart! He was double promoted twice. Always said he'd make something of himself, and he did, I guess."

"Yeah," my mother said, but she didn't sound too sure.

I knew that I shouldn't be listening, but it was about my father. I had to hear it.

"But you know what?" my aunt whispered. "He was no happier than any of the rest of us. Less, I'd say. We've always had the land and each other. Poor Albert always wanted more. More money. More things. Always wanting, never having."

There was a moment of silence. Then my aunt continued. "But Jason isn't like my brother."

I'm not like my father! The words stung. For my whole life, my father had told me how lucky we were, how many things I had compared to him when he was growing up. I no longer felt so lucky.

"Jason is thriving here," my aunt continued. "It was a little rough at first, but he's doing fine now. Better than fine. He's one of us, and that means more than all the money in the world."

One of us. Why did those words make me feel so good?

Chapter 18

I SHOULD HAVE GONE SLEDDING, I thought, lifting another shovelful of snow and carrying it to the side of the clearing. Alice and Billy were there with me, but Sally, Henry and George had gone sledding with Jeannie. And those guys would be here tomorrow, skating on this ice after doing none of the work. It wasn't fair.

Some of the other kids were there at the pond too. Guy and Ross DuBois had come. Other than Guy and Billy, J.B. was the only other of the older boys who was shoveling. Ricky was there from my group. We had been shoveling for almost two hours and had cleared an area that was only about half as big as a hockey rink.

The wind was whipping across the ice, often blasting icy snow crystals into my face and eyes. The sky was gray and threatened to snow more. I prayed that it wouldn't. My hands and face were cold, but the rest of my body was so warm that my underclothes were soaked with sweat. Shoveling was hard work.

"Break time," Guy hollered. Guy had taken charge of the shoveling effort. No one had elected him boss, but he just took command and people did what he said. "Come on over for lemonade."

Guy shuffled over the newly cleared ice surface and sat down on a bank of snow. He passed out plastic cups, and everyone took turns filling their cups from his two gallon camping jug.

I pressed the button, holding my cup underneath the spigot, filling it to the top. I released the button, and the last drips of lemonade overflowed onto the ice. I looked down and giggled to myself. The yellow liquid on the ice did not look like lemonade.

I sat down next to Guy and Ross and brought the cup to my lips. The ice cold drink was sweet in my mouth and slid down my dry throat. Boy did that hit the spot! In a second I had chugged my entire cupful.

"Aah," I said and turned to Guy. "Thanks."

"I'm glad you came, Jason. Not the most exciting way to spend a Sunday afternoon, but another two hours and we'll have enough ice to skate on tomorrow after school."

"It'll still be pretty small if we have to break up into two games," I said.

Guy nodded.

"And the kids who aren't here today will have a pretty good deal," I added.

"You're right. It's not really fair. But if the temperature gets into the teens for the next few nights, my dad might come and plow a bigger area for us."

Guy looked at me holding my empty cup and said, "Go ahead. Have some more."

"Thanks." I refilled the cup and was putting it to my lips when...Splash! The lemonade was all over my face!

I glanced up and saw Billy standing twenty feet away, hands held high in celebration.

"They call me Pedro Martinez!" Billy said to Alice just as I realized that Billy had nailed my lemonade with a snowball.

Billy turned to the imaginary crowd and bowed to the left and then to the right. He turned his back to me and did another bow when a snowball went flying through the air and exploded on the seat of Billy's pants.

Standing next to me, Guy lifted his fist in celebration. "Yeah, good target!" he said, referring to Billy's butt.

Alice and Billy sprinted to the nearest snow bank, about fifteen feet from Guy, Ross and me. Alice and Billy grabbed at the snow and furiously began forming snowballs. J.B. was near the lemonade jug and so he joined Guy, Ross and me. Ricky found himself sided with Billy and Alice.

In seconds snowballs filled the air, flying back and forth. I wound up and fired one at Alice which knocked the wool hat clean off her head! But I was too late to notice Ricky on the attack as I felt a small snowball explode right on my mouth.

"Huddle!" Guy cried. Guy, me, Ross and J.B. formed a tight circle, ignoring the high snowballs being hurled at us.

"Listen," Guy said. "We have a man advantage. Let's make use of it. Jason, make three snowballs, and when I say go, attack from the right. Don't throw your snowballs too soon. Ross, you do the same thing from the left. Once you guys start to throw, J.B. and I will attack from the middle and destroy them when they're looking at you. Set?"

We all nodded. The four of us carefully built sturdy snowballs, and then Guy said, "Now!"

Ross attacked from the left, and I charged from the right, both of us hooting and screaming while keeping our faces down. A snowball pounded the top of my head and another got me in my stomach, but I didn't slow down. Then I hummed my first snowball. When Ross saw me fire, he began to throw his snowballs. Alice, Billy and Ricky were busy looking to their left and then to their right when J.B. and Guy fired perfectly aimed fastballs at them. All three of them were hiding their faces in their arms as I ran right up to Billy. When Billy finally peeked up, I let him have it with my last snowball!

"Surrender!" J.B. commanded.

Alice, Billy and Ricky threw down their snowballs and held their hands in the air.

"Nice job, gentlemen," Guy said to J.B., Ross and me.

All seven of us returned to the lemonade where we filled our cups and bragged about our great throws.

"Good fight, cuz," Billy said to me as we resumed our shoveling.

It was going to be a long afternoon, but the snowball fight had been a blast and I felt full of energy. We were a group of seven, working hard with a tough job to do. And I was a part of the group. It was a good feeling.

Chapter 19

"IT'S ME, ROSS, JASON and Ricky against Billy, Alice, and J.B.," Guy announced as the gang of kids put on their skates. "The rest of you guys can take turns subbing in on Billy's team to make it a four on four. Okay?"

"What are we supposed to do when we're not playing?" George asked.

"There's not enough room for more kids to play. So I brought all those shovels for the rest of you to dig out a bigger area for us to skate on."

"That sounds like a lot of fun," Gary grumbled. Gary was a friend of Billy's and Guy's.

"Oh, shoveling is great fun," Guy answered sarcastically. "Ask any of us who spent all afternoon out here yesterday."

"Who was here?" Chad asked.

"Look at who's skating, genius," Guy replied, and Chad glumly shut his mouth.

"Maddy, you be on our team first," Alice said. "Then you can switch off with the other shovelers every ten minutes."

The kids who weren't playing all complained quietly, but no one dared defy Guy. A couple of the younger ones began untying their skates.

"Wait," I said. "Don't take off your skates. There's enough cleared ice now so you can shovel from the sides of it and keep your skates on while you do it. It'll be good edge practice!"

The younger kids smiled and began to retie their skates or get help from the older kids if they couldn't do it themselves.

Guy set up the goals and said, "You guys take it out first."

Alice stick-handled the puck and sent a sharp pass left to Maddy. Maddy couldn't handle it cleanly, and while she tried to regain control, Ross flew in and smacked the puck away.

"Alice, what are you passing to Maddy for?" Billy complained. "J.B. and I are on your team!"

Alice said nothing as I streaked behind Ross on the bumpy ice and picked up the loose puck and tried to take it around J.B.. The ice was terrible! The worst that I had ever skated on. I lost control of the puck and was about to complain about the lousy ice when I thought better of it. They'd think I was just a spoiled city boy again. Besides, the ice was crummy for both teams. I kept my mouth shut and came to a stop. Then I sprinted back to help out on defense. Maddy had the puck for them and she and Alice were skating toward our goal. Only Guy was back on defense for our team. Maddy began to take the puck to the left around Guy, but Guy was bigger and faster. He accelerated to his right, skating backwards, and began to turn his body to the side to force Maddy away from the goal. At the moment Guy turned, Maddy slipped a perfect pass across the center, right on the stick of Alice. It was a perfect 2-on-1 play, just the way I had showed them!

"Yes!" I said quietly, and then remembered that Alice and Maddy were on the other team. Alice scored easily, but I was still proud of them. I noticed Billy looking surprised and impressed.

"One zip, you're ahead," Guy announced.

"We don't usually keep score," Alice said to Guy. "But you do what you like. We're just going to play."

Guy looked confused. He'd probably never played without keeping score before. But he didn't say anything. Guy picked up the puck and slid an easy pass to his little brother who began skating up ice. As Billy charged Ross, Ross faked to his left and pulled the puck to the right, easily going by Billy. Billy's mouth dropped. He was shocked. Little six year-old Ross had just deked big fourteen year-old Billy out of his skates! It was awesome.

Ross instantly passed ahead to me. I had clear sailing into the goal but looked up anyway while I skated in. Guy was on my right. I shuffled a short back-hand pass to Guy who one-touched it right back to me. I shot it through the boots for a score.

"Great play, you guys!" Guy cheered. "That was really beautiful. We're passing like the Russians!" In international play, the Russian team was known for its disciplined passing attack.

The game continued, back and forth, with a different shoveler substituting in every ten minutes with Billy, Alice and J.B.. It was a close game, but still Guy stopped keeping score after a while. The shovelers rested a lot and watched the game. I loved to see the surprise on the faces of the older boys when one of my girls or younger boys made a beautiful play. And there were lots of them. The only bad part of the game was that the pucks kept getting stuck in the snow along the banks. We even lost two of them that way. Guy said that once the banks freeze it will be much better. But it was great, soft banks and all. Even though the ice was horrible, I had so much fun.

It was so dark that we could barely see when we quit for the afternoon.

"I can't believe how good you kids gave gotten!" Guy said, unlacing his skates. Some of the other older boys nodded as well, though they didn't look too excited about it. "And Jason, you played an awesome game. You really are a puckster."

The kids all looked at me, and I smiled.

"I never heard of a puckster before," I said. "They don't use that term back home."

"Actually, they don't use it up here much these days either. My father uses it, though. They used to say it around here when he was a kid. A puckster is a kid who lives for hockey: eats, drinks and sleeps it, and is very good too."

"I do love playing," I said.

"My brother Ross has really had a great time skating with you down here this month. He told me he's learned a lot. How'd you like to play with us older kids again?" Guy asked.

My heart leapt! It was what I had wanted so badly just a month ago. But then I looked at the faces of my skaters. Ross gazed up at me with wide eyes as if he were ready to cry. With raised eyebrows and a down-turned mouth, Ricky looked nervous and sad. Sally frowned. Alice looked eagerly at me, trying to read my response, but she hid her feelings well. Alice's friend Maddy looked hurt.

"We could really use you against Mill Creek this year. What do you say?" Guy asked.

I didn't know what to say. I had heard so many kids at school talk about the big game against Mill Creek. The Mill Creek kids thought they were better than the Glenville kids, and the Glenville kids wanted to win badly. Especially Guy.

But I was drawn again to the faces of my skaters, my "team" as I had begun to think of them. I'd feel like Benedict Arnold if I abandoned them. I didn't want to be a traitor. Plus, I loved to play each day with them. And they were learning so much.

"I can't," I finally said. "These other guys are my team. Sorry."

"Fair enough," Guy said, trying to mask his disappointment. "If you change your mind, you're welcome to play with us. We'd love to have you."

"Thanks," I said, feeling really good deep down.

One by one, the kids turned away from the pond and walked over the frozen ground. Horns were honking from cars with parents waiting to take their children home.

Chapter 20

"JUST ME AGAINST YOU," I challenged my cousin Billy. "Then we'll go sledding."

"Okay," Billy said, "for the championship."

All of my cousins gathered around the domed hockey game to see the final challenge match. Billy and I were the two best in the family. We'd soon see who was tops.

"You ready?" Billy asked.

"Definitely," I said with a confident smile, the same smile that Billy had flashed me before the end of that mini-basketball game.

"Come on, Billy," George encouraged his older brother.

"Let's go, Jason," Alice cheered her cousin.

"Yeah," echoed Henry, Sally and Jeannie.

"First one to get three goals wins," Billy announced.

"Fine. I'll be red," I said as Billy pressed the button to drop the puck.

Billy flicked his center and won the face-off. He pushed his left wing forward with the puck on his stick. Billy no longer just flicked the puck wildly up ice the way he used to. He now played a smart, controlled game. I had my right defenseman in position when Billy slid a perfect pass to his center who fired a shot at my goal. It looked like a beautiful shot but just skittered wide. I bit the side of my mouth to suppress my grin.

"Yay!" Sally and Henry cheered.

My defenseman scooped up the puck in the corner and flung a length-of-the-ice shot past Billy's goalie.

"Yeah!" Alice cried, clapping.

I loved having most of the fans on my side. A home ice advantage.

The play went back and forth, with Billy's goalie making some great saves. Billy shot two other pucks right at open spaces in my net, but they seemed to change direction at the last minute. At least it looked that way to me. The net was small, and so just the tiniest direction change could divert a potential goal. And the puck was traveling so fast, it would be almost impossible to detect.

Finally, I jammed in my center on a breakaway, scoring my second goal.

"Drop the puck," Billy growled, getting madder by the second.

The puck bounced off the plastic ice surface and started to roll toward my goal. Billy furiously flicked his players, pushing them in and pulling them out, but he could not score a goal. Finally, a lucky deflection skipped by Billy's goalie, and I had won, 3-0.

"Hooray!" Alice, Henry, Sally and Jeannie cheered.

Billy just stared in disbelief at the table hockey game. He finally looked up, smiled politely and extended his hand. "Nice game, Jay," Billy said.

I felt guilty but shook his hand anyway. Firmly.

"Let's go out sledding now," Billy said.

"Yeah," Henry agreed, and the others echoed the same thing.

One by one they left the room, heading down to bundle up for the bitter cold outside. Henry was the last to leave when he turned around and looked at me funny. "You all right? I thought you'd be happy to win."

"Yeah," I said, and a smile crept across my face.

"What is it?" Henry asked.

"Remember when Billy taped the mini-basket?"

Henry laughed. I had showed the basket to him later that day when we were alone. "Uh-huh."

"Well, this was my turn."

"What do you mean?" Henry asked.

I pressed the puck release button and grabbed the puck out of the plastic pocket. I dug my fingernails into the sides of the lightweight puck and suddenly it was in two pieces. I turned one half upside down onto the palm of my hand and picked up a small black metal-like chunk and handed it to Henry.

"What is it?" Henry asked.

"A magnet."

"What does that do?"

I turned the big domed table hockey game onto its side, and peeled a large magnet off the bottom from beneath my goalie. It had been taped on.

"So what does that do?" Henry asked again.

"The north poles of two magnets repel each other. I learned it at a science museum near where I live. Put a magnet on a table, and try to touch it with the same kind of magnet. You can't do it. One of them will push the other away without touching it."

"Oh, I get it," laughed Henry. "That's awesome!"

"Yeah," I chuckled, "but I felt kinda bad about winning that way, you know, with all you guys cheering me on and everything."

"Jason, that was against Billy! After all he's done to you!"

"I know, but he had made such a big deal about the game. Plus I know that I could have beaten him fair and square. And he was a good sport about losing. He even shook my hand."

Henry sighed. "Yeah, I know what you mean. Just play him again."

"I will," I said.

"Let's go sledding now!"

We ran downstairs, wrapped ourselves in layer after layer of warm clothing and headed out. We walked to Humbert's Hill, about a half mile away. It was too snowy for Aunt Susan to drive. Dean Run had the best sledding but was too far away if we had to walk. The bitter winds stung my face, and my hands and feet quickly became very cold. It was only my cousins and I there. We had a toboggan, a Flexible Flyer that must have been fifty years old, and Jeannie's snow tube, her Christmas present last winter.

Each of us took turns using all the sleds, and we had a blast. Henry and I usually went down together. Once, all seven of us squeezed onto the toboggan and slid down the hill. We couldn't move our arms to steer it, and so the toboggan turned around backwards and hit a bump, flipping over completely. I ended out on the bottom of the pile, smothered by all six of my cousins on top. But the snow was soft, and I was well padded with clothing. It was pretty funny.

Sally complained about the cold first, and I was relieved when Billy said, "Okay, why don't we go now." No one disagreed.

Trudging back to the house was painful. By the time we got there I couldn't even feel my feet or hands. Stepping into the house, I ran to the roaring orange blaze in the fireplace and peeled off my mittens. I held my hands up to the flames and they hurt even more but it felt good, too. I had never been so cold in my life. I wondered if I had frostbite. I'd seen pictures in magazines of people with frostbite. Their fingers or face or toes always turned black. I had read that they sometimes fall off afterwards. I didn't want that to happen. If I lost some fingers, how would I hold a hockey stick?

My cousins and I all huddled around the fire, slowly removing our outer clothing and dropping it all in a heap in the middle of the room.

Aunt Susan came in. "Pick up your clothes, then there's cocoa in the kitchen." We stayed by the fire for a few more minutes, then dug through the clothes, found our own and hung them in the well swept back hall.

While we sipped the hot cocoa, Billy stared at me and said, "Rematch?"

I nodded.

"Jason, you beat him fair and square! Don't play him again. Let's play teams, like we usually do," Alice said.

"Naw, I think that I need to play him."

"Why?" Alice asked. "He wouldn't play you again if he had won."

I ignored her and just sipped at my cocoa. It was piping hot but felt awesome as it trickled down my throat. And the sweetness of the melted marshmallow was delicious. Even holding the hot mug felt great on my still frozen hands.

When I was finally finished, I thanked Aunt Susan and headed upstairs. All six of my cousins followed.

"Ready?" Billy asked.

"Let me show you something first," I said.

I handed Billy the split puck and the small piece of magnet. Billy examined the pieces carefully in his hand. "What's this?" he asked.

"That's the puck we used earlier."

"Huh?"

"And that's a magnet I put inside. I did it yesterday and glued it together with a glue stick. Then I taped another piece of magnet, a really big one, beneath my goalie. Two magnets repel each other."

"And so the puck wouldn't go in the goal," Alice said, with an 'aha' in her tone.

"Exactly."

"Why, you..." Billy started angrily.

"I thought that it was an even better trick than taping the top of the mini-basketball rim," I said.

Billy's jaw dropped in surprise. "You knew?" he asked.

"Yes."

"And you didn't say anything?"

"I thought that it would be more fun to get even."

"And you sure got even," George chuckled admiringly.

"You did," Billy conceded, grinning himself. "So let's have the real thing now."

"You got it," I said, dropping the puck.

I couldn't keep up with Billy's quickness. My cousin had learned all of my strategies and used them against me. Plus, I couldn't get my mind off the great trick I had played on Billy. I couldn't stay focused on the game at hand. In ten minutes, the contest was over. The score was 3-1. I had lost.

I shook hands with Billy and said, "Nice game." Still I couldn't help but feel like the real winner today. I had outsmarted my fourteen year-old cousin.

Chapter 21

CHRISTMAS EVE HAD ALWAYS been the longest day of the year for me. And it would be even longer this year. For one thing, I was more excited about Christmas than ever. In the past, the best part had been thinking about what I would be getting for presents, and I usually knew what the big gift would be. But this year, at the Reese's, Christmas would be extra special. It's funny, I thought, and this will probably be the first year that I won't get what I asked for. I was almost sure that I wouldn't get the Canadian Hockey Tour that I so badly wanted. But I had been getting used to the idea. I was actually getting almost as excited about playing for Glenville in their annual game against Mill Creek.

For the past three weeks, I had played with Guy and the older boys at least once a week, on Fridays, and sometimes Saturdays for a couple of hours too. Alice and Maddy ran scrimmages with the younger kids at those times. Guy had even asked me to teach the older boys a few things, so I had run drills for about twenty minutes each day before we played our game. Some of the kids, like Guy and J.B., were eager to learn new things. It was obvious that they were practicing the skills that I was teaching them. They would barely be able to do a move when I taught it on Friday, yet by the following week those two would always have it down pat.

Even my own game had improved. My game instincts were much sharper. It made sense, though. I figured that in two hours of pick-up pond hockey with no subs, I got as much game time as I did in ten youth hockey games! Those youth hockey games were only thirty-six minutes, and a team had three lines to play. That's just twelve minutes of playing time a game.

Unfortunately, it was so warm out that there was no skating today. A heat wave before Christmas! I prayed that there would be no warm spell during February vacation. That would mean canceling the big game against Mill Creek.

I sat alone on the front steps, thinking about hockey. It seemed pretty cold today. They should let the kids skate. I was sure that the ice was safe. But Mr. Bailey had posted the No Skating sign again this morning. A school principal had to play it safe. They'd sue him if someone went through and got hurt. He'd probably get fired too. He was a good guy, though, and so I tried not to be angry with him.

And then my thoughts bounced back to Christmas. The Reeses had a huge tree in their living room which they had let me pick out and cut down myself. It was the first *real* tree that I had ever had. My mom and dad always had a fake Christmas tree, though my mother constantly reminded me that it was the most realistic looking fake tree you could buy. And they had paid enough for it, she'd say. I used to spray the 'tree smell' stuff on it so that it would smell like a real tree, but that spray made it smell more like a bathroom than an actual pine tree. Now this tree, this was different. My favorite thing about the tall full pine tree was the deep, refreshing evergreen smell. I sniffed it all the time. My cousins constantly made fun of me for putting my nose right up to the tree and taking a big whiff. Billy said that I was trying to get high on pine sap. But it didn't bother me. I just laughed with them. I knew that they were all pleased that I loved their tree so much.

Under the tree were loads of presents. Everyone had gotten everyone else a present in the family. Including me and my mother, that was ten people! No one had much money to buy expensive presents, but everyone had either made or found something for everyone, or bought something inexpensive.

I loved the stockings hanging over the fireplace. There was one for everyone in their family, even Aunt Susan and Big John, plus ones for my mother and me. Aunt Susan had sewn beautiful Christmas designs on everyone's stockings with their name stitched in fancy script at the top. For my mother and me, there were just big white socks. The one with blue stripes was mine, and the plain one was my mother's. I had insisted that they use one of Big John's socks for me because it was so big it would hold lots of candy. Aunt Susan had laughed and agreed.

Christmas with the Reese family meant staying up late to go to midnight Mass on Christmas Eve. Aunt Susan said that we would go to the French Mass. I was getting used to the church. I pretty much knew when to stand, kneel and sit, but I still sometimes got mixed up when we went to the French Mass.

And Henry and George told me that Christmas Day meant eating candy from the stockings, opening presents, playing with toys, and then playing outside. They said that the whole family usually went sledding if there was snow. And dinner was always a turkey, the biggest they could find. All the meat you could eat was a treat in the Reese house. Turkey with gravy, and lots of it, made my mouth water. Aunt Susan had been busy making her own cranberry sauce, and my cousins said that her stuffing was the best in the world.

Footsteps sounded behind me, and I turned my head. It was Billy, carrying a brown paper bag.

"Where you going?" I asked.

"Spy Pond."

"Skating?"

"Sh!" Billy said, nodding.

"But it's closed," I said.

"It's cold enough," Billy whispered. "I'm going there with George and Guy. Want to come?"

"Sure!"

"Get your skates, but don't let my mom or dad see."

I quickly smuggled my skates out in a paper bag and ran into George doing the same. Everyone else was too busy to notice, it being Christmas Eve.

In minutes, we were on our way to the pond. It was a long walk, but I didn't mind. It wasn't too cold. When we got there, Guy was already skating.

"See, it's great!" Guy said, gliding on the smooth surface.

The ice looked a lot better than before the warm spell. The surface had melted and refrozen, and it looked like glass, almost like the first time I had skated on it.

I quickly put on my skates and laced them, tying them as tightly as I could.

"You want me to pull them tight?" Billy asked.

I nodded. Billy could make them much tighter than I could. He pulled the ends of my laces so hard that my ankles almost hurt, but I liked my skates on snug. They felt good that way. Like my dad used to tie them.

Then we were all on the ice. Billy was the biggest, and when he skated past the 'No Skating' sign, I could hear the ice crack. I felt a surge of panic!

Guy laughed. "Don't worry, Jason, it always cracks when you're the first ones out and no one's skated on it for a long time. It's air pockets underneath, just settling."

I felt relieved, but only a little.

"Just stay away from those edges on the north side of the pond," Guy said to me, pointing to the benches about a rink's length up the side to our left. "The pond is fed through there, and so the ice is thinnest around that spot."

Guy set up the goals and said to George, "Me and Jason against you and Billy." Guy usually chose to have me on his side. It made me proud.

Guy took out the puck and sprinted with it up the ice and to the right. George streaked after him and knocked it away. Billy skated over and picked up the loose puck but I was on him and immediately poke-checked the puck off his stick. I sprinted after the puck, again hearing the crack of the ice. I didn't like that sound at all.

"Slow down!" Guy yelled. "That's the thin..."

I didn't hear the next word. I heard a split unlike any I had heard before. The ice just opened up, and I was completely enveloped in the frigid water. Never had I felt a jolt like that cold water surrounding me. I was a strong swimmer. I had taken lessons each summer at camp since I was three. I opened my eyes for a second to see which way was up, then I let go of my stick and tried to swim to the surface but my head smacked into something hard. The ice! I was trapped under the ice!

I was getting colder and I couldn't hold my breath much longer. My lungs were ready to burst. My eyes stung when I opened them again, but I needed to find the hole in the ice. I hoped that it hadn't refrozen. Then I saw it, just a few feet away. My arms could barely move they were so numb with cold, but I gave it everything I had. My head burst through the surface of the water, and I sucked huge amounts of air into my lungs.

"Help!" I cried.

I saw Guy and George and Billy lying flat on the ice, with Billy closest to me, holding out his hockey stick.

"Grab it, Jason!" Billy yelled, half commanding, half begging.

I reached my arm forward, but it could barely move. Billy inched his way towards me, extending his stick further, just inches away from my outstretched hand.

"Reach!" Billy yelled.

"I can't!" I cried, but I did reach a little farther. My hand was on the stick now.

"Grab hold!"

But my fingers couldn't move. They were too cold. My leg muscles stopped moving too. 'Oh no,' was all I could think. Then my head slipped back under the water. Blackness came next.

Chapter 22

WHEN I OPENED MY EYES, I saw my mother and Aunt Susan gazing down at me and smiling. My mother's eyes were puffy and red. Aunt Susan looked even worse, her eyes filled with tears.

"Jason, dear," my mother said, "are you all right?"

I nodded, then looked around the bright, white room. I was in a hospital! I tried to remember what had happened. What was I doing here? Where was I last?

"Merry Christmas, Jason," Mom said between sobs.

Christmas! It had been Christmas Eve, and I had been playing hockey with the guys. And I fell through the ice. That's all I remembered.

"Say something, dearie," Aunt Susan said kindly. They were both sitting on my bed, right next to me. I felt a hand in mine. I knew from the short stubby fingers that it was Aunt Susan's. I squeezed it.

"Merry Christmas, Mom. Merry Christmas, Aunt Susan. It's Christmas today?"

They both nodded.

"How did I get out of the ice?"

"Billy did it," my mother said and cried some more. She got a hold of herself and added, "Billy jumped into the water and pulled you up. He pushed you up onto the ice, and Guy and George pulled you safely away."

"What about Billy?" I asked.

Neither woman could say a word.

"He's still unconscious, Jason," my mother said to me.

"He'll be okay, though, right?"

"We don't know yet," Mom said. "We hope so."

"I'm so glad you're all right," Aunt Susan said, still weeping.

"Where is Billy now?" I asked.

"He's in intensive care," Mom said.

"Why aren't you with him?" I asked my aunt.

"I have been. Constantly. But they just told me that you were coming out of it. I needed to see you."

I thought about Billy in intensive care. I didn't know what intensive care really was, but it didn't sound good. "He might die?" I asked.

"We hope not," my mother said calmly. She paused for a moment before adding, "Why were you out there?" There was a hint of anger in her voice now.

"I'm sorry, Mom. We thought it would be safe."

"Ellen," Aunt Susan said, "it's all right. It was an accident. Boys will be boys. Accidents happen."

Just then a nurse walked into the room.

"We're awake at last," the older nurse said in a deep, almost manlike voice. "I told you not to worry," she said to my mother and aunt. "His signs were good. He just needed a rest. He'll be as good as new in no time."

"What about Billy?" I asked the nurse.

"I don't know, but I think that he'll come through. We should know any time. They usually pull out of these things in a day or so."

"Are his signs as good as mine?" I grilled her.

She didn't answer.

"Please, tell me!" I insisted and began to cry. Why had I gone skating yesterday? And why did I skate after that puck when it went along the north shore? I desperately wished that I could do it all again, do it more smartly.

Suddenly, in burst Big John.

Breathless, he blurted, "He's moving! They think he'll make it!"

My mother and aunt hugged each other tightly and cried some more. Big John came over to me and said, "Good to see you, boy. I'm sorry my Billy talked you into going to the pond. George told me all about it."

"He didn't talk me into it. He just asked me. He's going to be okay, isn't he, Big John?"

"Yeah. I'm going to get back to him. Alice is there with him now. When he wakes up, he'll be glad that you're okay."

"Big John!" I called out.

My uncle turned around.

"He saved my life," I said in a quivery voice.

Big John quietly said, "*Oui.*" He nodded to me and left the room with Aunt Susan.

Within two hours, they were letting me roam the corridors in a wheelchair. It was fun! There weren't many people at the hospital. It being Christmas, only the sickest people had to stay, so I had the corridors almost to myself. An hour later, they let me wheel my way down to see Billy. Billy couldn't talk, but his eyes were open and he smiled at me.

In my own room two hours later, I awaited dinner. Hospital food! Some Christmas dinner, I thought. Some Christmas. But at least I was alive, and so was Billy. It had been a close call, but we were here.

George had just told me that they had moved Billy out of intensive care, and he was sitting up now and even talking a little. That made me happy. George explained how he and Guy were able to hook a hockey stick under Billy's jacket and pull him up and out of the water as if they were fishing. But Billy had swallowed too much water and was unconscious like me. George had run to get help while Guy had done mouth-to-mouth resuscitation to both me and Billy. Guy's mother was a nurse and she had insisted he learn CPR. That was lucky for us.

"Hello," Mom said, walking into my hospital room. "Time for Christmas dinner."

"Here?" I asked.

"In Billy's room."

I got out of bed and sat on my wheelchair. Mom began to push when I said, "I can do it myself."

I led the way to Billy's room. Everyone in the Reese family was there except for Aunt Susan.

"Merry Christmas! Merry Christmas!" they all said to me.

"Merry Christmas, everyone," I answered, beaming. "Merry Christmas, Billy."

"Merry Christmas, Jason," he croaked in a frog-like whisper.

Aunt Susan entered the room pushing a hospital cart piled high with food.

"I know that you kids probably want to open presents, and we always do that first, but I've been working on this meal for three days and I'm not going to serve it cold."

No one argued with Aunt Susan. The food smelled delicious! I realized that I was starving.

Aunt Susan began serving her home-cooked food on plastic hospital plates. There was a pile of sliced turkey which made my eyes almost pop out of my head. She gave me one slice.

That's all? I thought that this was an all-the-meat-you-could-eat meal?

It was as if Aunt Susan could read my thoughts. "There's plenty here, but the doc said to go at it slowly. You haven't eaten in a day, and if you have too much, it'll come up on you."

The kids all suppressed grins.

I didn't want to throw up, and so I happily took my single slice. Big John gave me a small scoop of mashed potatoes, a dollop of stuffing and some green beans. He added a spoonful of cranberry sauce on the side.

No one began eating until everyone was served.

"Merry Christmas," Aunt Susan declared.

The whole family echoed "Merry Christmas" and started to eat. I sat in my wheelchair, wearing a skimpy hospital robe called a johnny. Big John and Aunt Susan sat on Billy's bed with him. George and Alice sat on the empty bed in the room and the rest of the kids just sat on the floor. I put the first bite of turkey to my lips. Awesome. Christmas dinner was everything I had hoped for.

Chapter 23

FLASH! WITH HIS NEW camera, Henry snapped a picture of his sister opening her gift.

"Do you like them, Sally?" I asked eagerly.

"Yes, thank you," Sally said, ripping the last of the Santa Claus wrapping from her new hockey skates. "They're the best skates I've ever seen!"

"They were my skates two years ago, but I grew out of them. I only wore them for half a year, so they're practically new. And they're the best skates you can buy."

The white plastic mold around the black leather boot was still clean and bright. Sally squeezed the skate at the ankle. It didn't budge. "Wow! Does this mean my ankles won't sag?"

"They better not," I said.

"Jason, this is the best Christmas present I ever got. Thank you."

"Thank my mom, too. She drove all the way to Boston to get a lot of this stuff from storage. That's where I got the shin pads for Henry and the skates for Jeannie."

"What about my hockey gloves?" George asked.

"They were going to be mine to grow into. We got them at a big sale last year."

"So what will you do when you outgrow the gloves you wear now?"

"Oh, I'll get something. Don't worry. They'll probably have invented a new and better glove by then anyway. Quadruple flex thumbs or something."

"I love my helmet and face mask, Jason, even if I'll be the only one wearing one," Alice said. "I don't want to look like those guys in the hockey book you gave Billy. You know, all the ones with no teeth."

Billy flipped through his *One Hundred Years of Hockey* and held up a giant photo for everyone to see. It was a faded black and white close-up of a grinning hockey player proudly displaying a mouth with four missing teeth. Everyone laughed. I had gotten that book last year for my birthday and had passed it on to Billy for Christmas.

"And thanks for my cup, too," Billy said, referring to the protective hockey cup and supporter he had received as well. "And it looks like it fits. What were you doing with one this big?"

I thought quickly. "Oh, I outgrew it about two years ago," I said, and Billy, George and Henry all laughed. The grownups pretended that they hadn't heard. Actually, it had been my father's cup. He had gotten it to play hockey with me but had never used it. Nobody needed to know all that. Who would ever want to wear a dead guy's cup?

My parents always said that giving was more fun than receiving. I had never believed them, not until now. Having my cousins open up the gifts from me and seeing how much they loved them, well, it was even better than opening my own presents.

I looked down at my gifts. That big white sock of Big John's was supposed to have disappeared Christmas morning. Instead, an even bigger one was going to have taken its place over the fireplace. But because we were in the hospital, Aunt Susan had just given me my new stocking. It was beautiful. My name was embroidered at the top, and sewn below were two hockey skates surrounded by snowflakes. Aunt Susan had made it for me. The details on the skates were incredibly realistic. For many nights Aunt Susan had slipped my Super Custom 404's to her room and replicated every detail in fine stitchery. I loved having my

own stocking with the skates and snowflakes, even if outdoor
hockey is better when it is not snowing!

Big John had given me a book called *A History of Acadians in
the Lower Valley*. He said that it began with the migration of the
original French settlers from south-eastern France in the early
1600's and went up until about ten years ago when the book
was published. There was even a mention of the annual
Glenville/Mill Creek pickup hockey game! After just a few
months of living in Glenville, I was seeing myself as an
Arcadian, just like my cousins, my aunt, my uncle, their friends,
and my father. The book made me feel a part of something big. I
treasured it.

George had given me his favorite flannel shirt, one that I had
asked to borrow many times but he had always said no. Now I
would look like a real Maine boy. The cocoa mug which said
WORLD'S BEST COACH was from Alice. Next to the mug was a
hockey puck from Sally. She had found it in the snow at the
pond. It looked like one that I had lost earlier in the winter. I
loved it anyway. Billy had given me a new "Best of the Eagles"
CD, even though I had no CD player. And the CD was wrapped
in a new pair of hockey socks for me. On top of the CD's was an
unopened pack of hockey cards from Henry. It even had a stick
of gum in it. And perched on top of my whole pile was a stuffed
bear from Jeannie. She told me that she gave it because she
"had a million of them." From the looks of it, that stuffed bear
had been given many times for Christmas.

"Has everyone opened everything?" Aunt Susan asked.

"Not yet," my mother answered. "Jason, Merry Christmas."
She handed me a huge wrapped present.

It can't be the Canadian Hockey Tour, I thought. That would
probably come in just an envelope. Unless she were tricking me
with the big box. Maybe she was. My dad had once given my
mom a diamond necklace wrapped in a huge box. Inside that

box was another box, and inside that another. She must have opened ten boxes before getting to the necklace.

I tore into the snowflake paper and ripped open a big carton inside. And then I recognized my old CD player and speakers which I had left in storage. And taped on top were five new CDs, all ones that I had wanted. I peeked to make sure that there was no envelope in there, too. I was happy to have the CD player and the new CDs. I tried hard not to look disappointed.

"I know what you wanted. I'm sorry. There wasn't enough money for the tour. I hope you like these." There was sadness in my mother's smile.

"Thank you," I said, hugging my mother and feeling bad that she felt bad. "Thank you so much," I whispered. "This is the best Christmas I ever had." And it was.

Then into the already crowded hospital room walked four adults followed by a gang of kids. I recognized some of the adult faces from the cars that dropped off the kids for hockey at Spy Pond. And then I saw Helena, Gina, Maddy, Danny, Ricky and Ross. It was my pond hockey team!

The smiles suddenly vanished from the kids' faces. They looked scared. I was wondering what it was when I noticed Ross's eyes glued to my wheelchair.

"Oh, the wheelchair," I said. "I'm all right, you guys. See?" I stood up. I was careful to hold the back of my johnny tightly together. The johnny was like a skimpy white apron, open in the back. I didn't want everyone to see my bare butt underneath. "They just give me the wheelchair to be extra safe. It's fun to whiz around in, so that's why I use it."

The children breathed a sigh of relief and most of them smiled again.

"Merry Christmas, Jason," they said, sort of at the same time. The hospital room was so crowded that I was worried that we might get into trouble. Luckily, Billy was in a two person room and the other bed was empty, so there was no one to bother and everyone could squeeze in.

Twelve year-old Maddy was the oldest of the kids, and she stepped to the front of the group and spoke. "Alice, Henry, Sally, come here. You're part of this, too." My three cousins squeezed their way through the crowd and joined their pond hockey teammates.

Maddy continued, "Jason, we're really glad that you're okay. We all chipped in for this present for you before you got hurt. We hope that you'll still be able to use it." Maddy handed me an envelope and said, "It's from all of us, the kids and our parents."

I took the large envelope from her. I was filled with curiosity and excitement as I ripped it open. I pulled out a huge, homemade card which said MERRY CHRISTMAS and THANKS FOR BEING SUCH A GREAT HOCKEY COACH. Ten hockey players were drawn on the front, one for each kid in the group plus me. Some of the players were beautiful, realistic sketches. Others were stark stick figures. Each kid must have drawn himself or herself, I thought. Looking at that card gave me a warm tingling feeling deep in my chest. It meant so much to me.

I opened the card and inside was a picture of a hockey goal and goalie, and underneath were the signatures of all nine kids.

"Thanks so much!" I said. It was beautiful.

"It's a pop-up card," Alice said. "Pull up the goalie!"

I grabbed the cardboard goalie and lifted him up. Underneath was a pocket with a folded piece of paper tucked inside. I took the light green paper and unfolded it. It was a check for seven-hundred dollars. I looked up, puzzled.

"It's for the hockey tour, stupid! The one this February!" Alice laughed.

"All the kids chipped in twenty-five dollars from their potato money," Sally piped in, "and our parents gave the rest, especially Ross's dad, who gave -"

"Sh! Sh!" Alice and Maddy both hushed Sally.

Holding the check, I looked up to my mother. "Is this enough for the tour, Mom?"

Watery-eyed, she nodded. "Close enough," she answered.

I couldn't believe it! I looked up at the glowing faces of Alice, Maddy, Henry, Sally, Gina, Helena, Ross, Ricky and Danny. I tried to say 'thank you' but the words would not come out. Tears rushed to my eyes. I tried not to cry, but those tears spilled out anyway. I was just so happy.

Chapter 24

I HAD NEVER BEEN SO excited for a hockey game. Or
nervous. I looked around the ice. There were actually spectators
here for this game. It was probably just the families of all the
players, but it had been a long time since I had played in front
of a crowd.

One of the best parts of youth hockey was playing games
inside rinks. When the parents screamed for a breakaway or a
goal or a great save, the sound magnified and echoed. It used to
sound like there were thousands of people screaming when in
reality there were probably only about twenty.

There would be no echoing here today. Sound does not carry
well outdoors. But at least it was cold and there was ice. It was
very cold, and the ice was hard and smooth.

I wore my blue Boston Hockey Camp shirt. Everyone from
Glenville was supposed to wear blue. The Mill Creek players all
wore various shades of red. I was sure that Glenville would win.
We had to win. But whatever happened, I knew that I had made
the right choice. Had I gone on the Canadian Hockey Tour, I
would have spent all week thinking about my friends in
Glenville, wondering how they were doing. If Glenville lost, I'd
never know whether I could have made the difference. Besides, I
wouldn't know anyone on the Hockey Tour. Even if we won the
tournament, I'd probably never see those kids again. I'd have
the trophy but nothing else. But these were my friends. And my
family. These were the people I wanted to play with. This was a
game I would remember forever and always have friends to talk
about it with.

And so I had used the seven-hundred dollars plus a little
from my mom to buy new hockey skates, good hockey skates,

for all of the players. Actually, not all of the skates were new. Most of the pairs had been bought from a second-hand store where you could get an excellent, almost new pair of hundred dollar skates for less than fifty bucks. When they hadn't had a certain size, we bought new skates. There was even enough money for me to buy my little kids each a decent pair of used skates.

My mother and Mr. DuBois, Guy and Ross's father, and Mr. LeClaire, J.B.'s father, had each driven with a car full of kids to Presque Isle for the purchases. I rode with Mr. DuBois. He had lost to Mill Creek three times when he was a kid. He passed the time on that long three hour car ride by telling us all about those games. Mr. DuBois badly wanted Glenville to win this year. He also talked about his family, his parents, grandparents, great-grandparents, and about how he was related to the original Acadian settlers to the valley in the late 1700's. And he talked a lot about the Acadian Festival they have each June. All the kids spoke excitedly about that event. I wondered how many generations of my family had lived in the valley. I decided then that I would go to the next Festival. I would insist that my mother drive me up for it. I didn't want to lose this group when I went back home. In Massachusetts, I was just Jason Quinn, hockey player. And on a different team each year. In Glenville, I was one of these people, one of these Acadians, and I would always be one. I was sad that my father had never felt this way, but my Acadian roots came from him, and I was thankful to him for it.

That shopping trip had taken place the week after Christmas. For almost two months now, the Glenville team had skated on real skates, and the improvement was unbelievable. I knew what a difference a good pair of skates makes. Everyone else now knew that too.

I had convinced Guy that Alice and Maddy were better than most of the boys in his group and that they should play on the Glenville team. Guy wanted to beat Mill Creek badly, and so convincing him hadn't been hard to do. The starting line-up was Guy, J.B., Billy, Alice and me. There were usually only a couple extras on each side, and so Guy had dressed Maddy, George, Gary and Chad as subs. Ross was also wearing blue and skating with our team. But even though he was good, he was only six and wouldn't play much, if at all. Guy figured that Ross would be the future of the Glenville skaters and wanted to give him a little big game experience. And Ross was his little brother. Plus, if tiny Ross ever deked one of the Mill Creekers, it would psyche them out badly.

I was glad that it was Glenville's turn to have the game on its ice. I had grown to love Spy Pond. And this would be my only winter up here to play in the game. My mother had settled my father's business affairs. We would be moving back to Massachusetts in June, where we would move to a smaller house in a different town. Mom would return to school for a year, and then get a job again as a nurse. I had mixed feelings about the move, but for now, I needed to concentrate on this game.

The ten of us skated in a circle on the ice, stick-handling pucks and secretly checking out our opponents at the same time. I loved my team. *Team.* I now knew what my coaches had been talking about.

The Mill Creek players were much bigger than we were. They must all be in the eighth grade, I thought. But I knew that age meant little. It was all in the skating, and Glenville could skate.

Guy had brought two broken hockey sticks for the goals. Boots sometimes got closer together or further apart, and this was too important a game to be determined by a net changing size. Both sticks were the same length. It would be fair. Guy slid one stick across the ice to where Mill Creek was warming up.

"Bo, here's your goal!" Guy hollered across the ice. Bo Hickey, the Mill Creek captain, waved and nodded as he skated for their goal stick. It would be the second time that Guy and Bo faced off as team captains. For each of them it would be their last Glenville/Mill Creek game. In minutes we were ready to play.

The two teams huddled near the center of the game ice. Bo and Guy shook hands.

"A little short on players this year," one Mill Creeker cracked, pointing to little me and tiny Ross. Most of the big Mill Creek skaters laughed.

"Let's just play hockey, guys," Bo said to his team. "Good luck, boys," he said to all of us, shaking Guy's hand.

"Bo, they're not all *boys*," another skater from Mill Creek called out, smirking at Alice and Maddy.

"Shut up!" Bo said sharply to his teammates. While the rest of the Mill Creek team looked cocky and relaxed, their captain cautiously eyed the Glenville skaters. He must have been watching us skate, I thought. I had noticed Bo Hickey skate. He was their best player. He clearly knew hockey. And so he knew that it was not going to be easy for Mill Creek this year.

"We play until one-thirty. No lifts unless a player goes down in front of the net. Right?" Bo said to Guy.

Guy nodded.

"I got noon. You?" Guy asked.

"Me too," Bo said. "Let's have a good game."

"Up or down?" Guy said, holding a new game puck.

"Up," Bo called.

Guy flipped the new University of Maine puck and it landed with the Black Bear side to the ice. "Down," he said, picking up the puck and carrying it behind his goal.

Chapter 25

AND WITH THAT FLIP of the puck, the game had begun. Guy skated up ice with the puck. He glided past J.B., who was starting in the goal. Guy successfully deked the first Mill Creek forechecker. Guy looked up and shuffled a quick pass to me. Without looking, I knew just where Alice would be. We had played together enough. I one-touched a pass to her on my right and she easily split the two Mill Creek defensemen. The Mill Creek goalie charged her. I knew that it was a mistake by their goalie. You'll get a weak player nervous if you charge him or her, but a skilled stick-handler will easily deke you and go by. Alice did just that. After passing their goalie she slowed down and carefully directed the puck into the empty Mill Creek goal. Glenville was ahead, 1-0 !

"Yeah, Alice!" I screamed, high-fiving her briefly but quickly dropping back into position.

"Nice pass, cuz" Alice said as we separated. Big John's voice roared above the cheering Glenville fans.

Bo Hickey led the red shirts back up ice. With good fakes he skated by the first two Glenville forwards, and tried to go around Billy as well. Billy was not agile on his skates, but he was strong and fast. He got his stick on Bo's and knocked the puck away. J.B. picked up the loose puck and slid it to me. I skated to my left with Guy on my right. The biggest Mill Creek player, a kid they call Tank, went flying full speed toward me. If I got hit by Tank, that would mean trouble. I wished that I had a helmet and face mask on, but none of the boys on Glenville or Mill Creek wore helmets. Only Alice wore one. Just before Tank got to me, I pushed off my right skate, moving sharply to my left. Tank tried to move with me, but he was not quick. He lost his balance and went crashing to the ice. I didn't turn around to see how far he slid or if he was okay. I was flying now and easily skated past the next red jersey. I looked up. Guy was still to my right. Bo Hickey was the only Mill Creeker back. Bo was covering Guy closely, too closely. Bo must have known how good Guy was. He probably didn't know about me, and so I faked a pass, causing Bo to pause a second, then I flew past him. My speed created a cold breeze whipping through my hair. I felt like Bobby Orr rushing the puck in the pre-helmet days. It was just me against the Mill Creek goalie now. He looked nervous. He was short and heavy, and probably their worst skater. I moved the puck to my left, then to my right, and from my backhand slipped the puck through the goalie's legs. It was 2 - 0 !

"Yay, Jason!" I heard Aunt Susan scream. All the Glenville fans were clapping and cheering. The families of all the players were there. The parents of the younger kids on my team were mostly at the game, too. There were even some Glenville fans that I didn't know. And they were all cheering us on.

Bo called his team together briefly. Glenville had scored two quick and easy goals. Mill Creek hadn't been expecting this, especially from a little kid and a girl. Now they knew what to expect. It was sure to get tougher.

Tank skated out with the puck for Mill Creek and passed to a short, fast kid with a Number 8 on his jersey. Alice attacked Number 8, but he quickly shuffled a pass back to Tank who streaked straight in on left wing. I skated backwards, face to face with Tank who approached me. No way can this big guy deke me, I thought. Tank stepped to his left and then slid a quick pass into the middle to his captain Bo. It was Bo against Guy, one-on-one, alone in the middle of the ice. Guy was skating backwards, stick held with one hand and extended out. And then Guy attacked. I knew that it was too soon. Bo easily carried the puck around Guy and sprinted to the goal. J.B. had dropped into the goal by this time, and he came out about ten feet to cut down on the angle. He was doing it right. J.B. correctly began to back into the goal slowly as Bo approached. Yes, I thought. Just right. Bo tried to deke left, but J.B. slid his skate over to make the save! The puck just sat there, five feet in front of an empty goal as momentum pulled J.B. and Bo to the side of the net. Suddenly Tank was there, and he fired the puck into the empty Glenville goal. The Mill Creek fans cheered. It was 2-1 .

That was my man, I thought angrily to myself. I'm supposed to pick up the trailer in that situation, but I didn't do it. I was too busy worrying about whether my teammates did their jobs. I can't do that, I told myself.

"Sorry, my fault," I said to Guy.

"I got beat. I blew it too," Guy said.

"Let me cover Bo," I suggested to Guy as we skated up ice. Guy hesitated. He looked torn. I knew that I was a stronger skater than Guy and could stay with Bo Hickey better. But Guy was the Glenville captain. What would it look like if he let someone else take on Mill Creek's captain and best skater?

"Okay," Guy finally agreed.

"Yes!" I said under my breath.

Glenville tried to advance the puck but this time Mill Creek was not charging us with all their players. They forechecked one player hard while the rest held back to let the Glenville skaters make the next move. There were no more easy dekes. Time after time, we brought the puck three quarters of the way up ice, but Mill Creek clogged the middle and played tough defense in front of their goal.

The Mill Creek offense, though, was having its troubles too. Their best play, setting up a one-on-one with Bo carrying the puck, was not working. I was quick enough on my skates that Bo could not fake me out. And when he went for raw speed, I had the jets to stop him. Each of the Glenville starters took a couple of short breaks, giving Maddy, George, Gary and Chad a chance to play. J.B. played great in the goal and wanted to stay there, and so he came out of the net only when we needed his speed with Guy or me on the bench. J.B was fast and could stay with Mill Creek's fastest skaters. But he was a great goalie, too.

I was impressed that we could play such an important game without any refs. Guy had told me that twice in the past the game had to be stopped because of arguing or fighting. *All* the players had been looked down upon by everyone in both communities. It was worse than losing, the skaters had all said later. There was now great pressure on the team captains to make sure that that never happened again. Guy and Bo took their responsibility seriously and had fairly settled the few small disputes so far.

It was around ten past one when Mill Creek's Number 8 snatched the puck off Danny's stick and went in alone on Billy who was playing the goal for us. Billy went down flat when Number 8 pulled the puck to the right. Number 8 lifted the puck over Billy and over the stick marking the goal.

"Lift! No goal!" Billy argued.

"You were down on the ice," Number 8 said. "I can lift it if you do that."

"He's right," Guy said to Billy. And so it was 2-2 .

Almost all of Glenville's shots were from about thirty feet out, and the Mill Creek goalie stopped them easily. Our only golden opportunity was when Guy threaded the needle with a gorgeous pass, feeding Maddy on a breakaway. Maddy flew in at the goalie, quickly moved the puck left and right and deked the goalie completely. But she lost control of the puck and it slipped just behind the goal.

"It's one-thirty!" Bo finally announced. The score was still knotted at two. According to Guy, there had never been such a low scoring game in the history of pickup hockey. Both teams respected the skills of their opponents and had played tight defensive games. There were no more comments about little kids and girls on the Glenville team. Even Ross, in his two minutes of ice time, had been treated with respect.

"Sudden death overtime," Guy said. "Next goal wins."

The starting five went out there for each team. Parents on both the Glenville side and the Mill Creek side shouted encouragement to their players.

For the first ten minutes of overtime, the defensive battle continued. Then Bo Hickey carried the puck up ice for Mill Creek. Billy charged, and Bo deked him easily. I waited at half ice. Suddenly Bo dug his skates into the ice and pushed off as hard as he could, coming toward me. He flew by Guy and Alice, and I knew that I was in trouble. It was as though Bo were putting everything he had into one last rush. I stopped skating backwards and turned to sprint toward my own goal. I dug in and gave it my all but Bo had more momentum and passed by me. Please, J.B., do it here, I begged silently. My goalie had to come through!

J.B. charged out of the goal and slid into Bo. Bo was going too fast to skate around him and still control the puck. It happened too quickly. They crashed just in front of me. I reacted quickly to avoid joining the pile on the ice and flew by them. Mill Creek's Number 8 was the trailer and steered the puck cautiously toward the open Glenville goal. J.B. brought his stick over his body, diving, and with one hand slammed his stick in front of the slow moving puck. The puck stopped. Another red shirted player streaked in and tried to lift the puck over J.B.'s stick which still lay flat on the ice. But he couldn't lift it and the puck bounced off the outstretched stick and rolled to the side of the net. I sprinted from behind my own goal and flew past the next Mill Creek trailer who was diving to knock in the rebound.

Boom! Boom! Boom! It was like a kamikaze attack by the Mill Creek forwards. But I had control of the puck. I turned up ice and looked to my left. Guy was there skating next to me. Back for Mill Creek, it was just big slow Tank on defense and their even slower goalie further behind.

Even in the open air, the screaming of the kids and parents on the side sounded like a crowd of thousands. I was pumped. Tank would back up on defense and see what I would do. If Tank leaned toward me, I would pass. Otherwise I'd blow by him on the right. Suddenly Tank charged right at me with all his speed and weight. I wasn't ready. Instinct told me to protect my face, but I'd lose the puck that way. I shuffled the puck blindly to my left, then wham! My face felt like it had shattered. I went down and whacked the back of my head on the ice. Ow! The pain was unbelievable.

The next thing I knew, I was lying flat on my back and slowly opening my eyes. My mother and Mr. DuBois were standing over me.

"Jason, you okay?" Guy's father asked.

"Did we score?" I asked through the pain.

Mr. DuBois smiled. "Yeah," he said, "Guy scored the goal. Thanks to your pass. You really are a puckster."

Guy skated over, joining his father, and he smiled down at me.

"We won?" I asked.

"Yes!" Guy said. "That was a great pass."

"On your stick?"

"Not exactly. In my skates, but no one was near me, and you taught me how to kick it up."

I wanted to smile, but the muscles in my aching face would not cooperate. I tried to get up but it hurt too much.

"Lie down," my mother told me.

But I wanted to be part of the winning celebration. I pushed as hard as I could with my arms and sat up. My head killed. My mouth ached. And then I noticed the blood splattered over my blue hockey jersey.

My Glenville teammates were celebrating with raised sticks. Mr. LeClaire, J.B.'s dad, was on the ice, keeping them away from me, but they were all cheering encouragement to me anyway. Despite my pain, a huge smile finally spread across my face.

"Oh my God," my mother said.

I saw a look of horror on her face.

"What's wrong, Mom?"

"Your front teeth!"

I moved my tongue to my front teeth. Actually to where my front teeth used to be. Nothing. I slid my tongue through a giant hole which felt as big as a baseball. Oh no, I thought. And one of them was a brand new second tooth!

"Baby teeth, I hope?" Mr. DuBois asked.

"Just one," my mother answered, shaking her head.

"It's not the end of the world," Guy's father said to my mom, pulling out a set of three false teeth from his mouth. "He'll ha' more teef 'an I do, hanks to Mill Creek," he garbled without his front teeth. "At 'east he won his game!"

My mother forced a smile to her face.

Mr. LeClaire saw that I was okay and let the team skate over to Guy and me. They all huddled briefly and whispered to Guy. And then Guy leaned over to hand something to me.

"I think you deserve the game puck. We couldn't have done it without you. It'll make a pretty cool trophy."

"Thanks," I said, my head starting to clear. "Just help me find my other two souvenirs."

"Huh?" Guy asked.

"My teeth!"

Everyone laughed. Then they all got on their knees and carefully ran their fingers through the thin layer of snow on the ice.

"I got one," J.B exclaimed.

"Oh, gross," Alice said. "I think I got one too." She held the tiny speck of tooth at arm's length between her thumb and index finger, looking away.

They each handed over a small bloody tooth to me. The teeth looked so tiny but the hole felt so big.

"Mom, I don't have any pockets. Hold on to all these?" I handed her the puck and my two teeth.

She raised her upper lip in disgust but held out her hand and took my three precious trophies.

Sitting on the ice I tried to absorb the whole scene. The fresh cold air felt good on my face and in my lungs. The majestic pine trees, the rocky cliff and the deep blue sky were breath-taking. The almost blinding reflection of the bright sun on the far end of the ice was spectacular. My eyes moved to our red jerseyed opponents, then to the cheering crowd, and finally to my joy-filled team, my friends. I wanted to memorize every detail. I knew then and there that this would be one of the most special moments of my life. I didn't want to forget any of it.

Epilogue

There is no doubt in my mind that it was that winter in Glenville which helped me most to get where I am today. And I was right. That magic moment, beating Mill Creek in sudden death overtime, is the single best memory I have from hockey. It was bigger than the state championship I won with my town Pee Wee team two years later. It was bigger than winning the national championship with the Black Bears.

Only one picture was taken that day on Spy Pond. So I'm glad that I worked so hard to memorize every last detail of that final moment. To this day, I can see, hear, feel and smell that scene as if it happened yesterday.

I went back home to Massachusetts that next summer. My mother worked with a lot of lawyers and straightened out our financial situation. We did lose most of our money, but there was enough left for us to get started again. I was relieved to find out that my father hadn't done anything illegal. He had made some poor decisions and had tried to hide it from us. He didn't want us to worry. So my mom returned to school for her nursing degree and then went back to work at a local hospital. We did move to a smaller house in a different town, and I went to the public school there.

They had a great hockey program, like my old town. I think my mother checked that out before deciding where we would move. I played youth hockey there but didn't play for the select team I had made the year before. I could have, but they flooded a field near our house, and I wanted time to play pickup hockey there. Whenever it was cold enough, I was there skating. Whenever it snowed, I was there shoveling. Sometimes I played with kids my own age or younger. And often I played with the older guys. I learned most of my best hockey moves by playing with the high school kids on that ice. I made a lot of friends there and had a whole lot of fun. And because it was only three feet at its thickest, my mother didn't worry. She did make me wear a helmet and face mask, though.

Every year after that winter, my mother took me for at least one visit to the Reeses. We'd go for either the Christmas or February vacation, and sometimes go in June as well for the Acadian Festival. As a result, I missed some youth hockey games for my Greater Boston League team, and some of my teammates weren't happy about that. But they never stayed mad for too long. George tried to get me to play against Mill Creek the following winter, but when they found out that I wasn't living in Glenville any more, the Mill Creekers said no. Mill Creek won the next two years, but the games were close. Alice was the star of the team that next year for Glenville. She went on to play hockey at Dartmouth College and was one of the Big Green's leading scorers. But when Ross was nine, he led Glenville to the start of their longest winning streak over Mill Creek in the history of the rivalry.

Ross turned out to be every bit as good a player as I had predicted, even better! He was a high school star and joined me at the University of Maine. In my senior year, that championship season, Ross was just a freshman, but he was the toughest and fastest defenseman on the team.

I'm playing minor league hockey in Canada now, and I hope that one day I'll play in the NHL. I have my degree in French, and I expect that after my playing days are over I'll end up teaching French or coaching somewhere. Maybe both. That book on Acadian culture from Big John started me on a quest to learn more about my own family history and about the heritage of my people from Northern Maine. I even thought about changing my name back to Quine, but I decided to stay with Quinn. My father chose that name, for himself and for me. To this day I travel to the Acadian Festival nearly every year and take special pleasure in getting to know my Quine relatives.

I still have my trophy from that Glenville/Mill Creek game. Big John mounted my game puck onto a beautifully carved stand and preserved the two teeth behind a tiny plate of glass in the stand. Right now I'm looking at my other memento of that game. Henry snapped the one picture taken that day. He had brought his new camera there but was too excited during the game and forgot all about it. He remembered it at the end of the game when he saw me smile, bloody and toothless. It reminded him of that picture in the book I had given Billy. Just when he was ready to shoot the picture, my mother had insisted that I clean the blood from around my mouth. Henry was using color film and so he was disappointed, but he wasn't going to argue with my mother. My mom used tissue to wipe away the blood. You probably can see the hole from the missing teeth better without all the blood anyway. And she didn't use water, so you can still see some red smudges at the corners of my mouth. I used to spend hours studying that photo. I'd gaze in fascination at the blood on my jersey and the traces of it on my face. I loved looking at the hole from the missing teeth, too. But now when I look at that photograph, I stare into the eyes of that boy. And in those eyes I see the pure joy of sports in a ten year-old's heart, and I remember why I play the game.

Mark Fidler lives in Waltham, Massachusetts with his wife and three sons. Besides teaching high school math and computer science, he has coached youth hockey and Little League baseball.

Also written by Mark Fidler –

Baseball Sleuth

Signed Ball

The Call of Sagarmatha

For more information about these books as well as new books soon to be published, turn to the following pages, or visit the author's web page at

www.markfidler.com

All books by Mark Fidler are on sale at most online bookstores. Or ask for them at your local bookstore.

How did you like *Pond Puckster?*
Tell the author! Email him at author@markfidler.com

Baseball Sleuth

By Mark Fidler

"You buried the body in the yard?"

These words, spoken to a man named Bob, crackle from the baby monitor. Phillip strains to hear more through the static. A murder! No one will believe him unless he finds out who Bob is, and where Bob lives.

Phillip Crafts loves baseball but he is a terrible player. He loves mysteries, but his teammates laugh at him when he sees crimes where they don't exist. Meanwhile, at home, his life is even worse. After twelve years of being an only child, Phillip's newborn sister has taken all of his mother's time, energy, and maybe even her love. And he is sure that he can never earn the respect of his "jock" stepfather. The only good thing in his life is his best friend Jackson, the girl next door.

Armed with few clues, Phillip and Jackson work to unravel the mystery of the buried body. Their investigation builds to an exciting and dangerous climax, just as Phillip's baseball season builds toward its final, dramatic game.

Signed Ball

By Mark Fidler

More than anything, eight-year-old Jimmy Jarvis wants a baseball autographed by his favorite major league player, and he is willing to do almost anything to get it. Jimmy has another wish, too. After living in six different foster homes in six years, Jimmy wants a family that will be his forever. But will he risk a chance at a real home for the ball of his dreams?

Follow Jimmy as he plots one wild scheme after another in his quest for that signed ball. And share the moving story of Jimmy's life as a foster child, where he faces choices that no young boy should have to make. Filled with humor and warmth, *Signed Ball* is a story the whole family will enjoy.

The Call of Sagarmatha

By Mark Fidler

Making diving headers on the soccer field or climbing the toughest walls of rock, Mardi Slote lives life to the fullest. Like her father, she fearlessly "pushes the envelope" in all she does. But when her father announces that he is going to climb the world's tallest mountain, a mountain that has already claimed more than a hundred lives, Mardi is afraid.

The Call of Sagarmatha follows David Slote's battle for survival against the elements on Mount Everest, or Sagarmatha, as the native people of Nepal refer to it. Meanwhile, Mardi must struggle with her anger, which threatens to destroy her zest for life, and tear her family apart.

In a novel which captures the drama of climbing, from the rocky cliffs of New Hampshire to the slopes of Mount Everest, the greatest struggle is in the soul of a twelve year-old girl. It's a battle that can only be won with the help of her family, her best friend Jeannie, her climbing partner Arthur, and her pen pal Ngwang, the young son of a Sherpa mountain guide.

Coming soon!

Blaze of the Great Cliff

By Mark Fidler

Above all else, young Blaze wants to be a man of his Sinagua tribe. He dreams of being a great hunter and warrior. But his people of the Great Cliff are a peaceful farming tribe and believe that learning the skills of war will anger the gods and worsen the drought that already threatens all the peoples of the desert. And then, on his first great journey, Blaze discovers the great Hohokam people and their game of guayball, a brutal and exciting sport played by both boys and men. Drawn to that culture which respects fighters above all others, Blaze must decide where his true spirit lies.

Enjoy the excitement, passion and danger of the final days of America's great cliff dwellings. In a world threatened by drought and war, one boy strives to grow up, and do the right thing for himself and his people.

Expected publication date: Fall, 2003

Coming soon!

Zamboni Brez

By Mark Fidler

An exciting novel about a season in the life of Stas Breznikov, a young Russian boy playing triple-A hockey in America. A big boy, Stas plays a very physical brand of hockey, but as the team loses, and Stas gets labeled a "goon," it seems that nothing can salvage the terrible season. Follow Stas as he struggles with life and hockey in his new country, and in the process, learns the secrets of his own father, a quiet man known as Zamboni Brez.

Expected publication date: Fall, 2003